DEAD-END TRAIL

Chet Rand is a decent, law-abiding man, but a forest fire wipes out his horse ranch, leaving him with nothing. However, when he comes across the outlaw Feeney — with a $1,100 reward on his head — it seems like a gift from heaven. Unfortunately, there are many shady characters in pursuit of the $12,000 Feeney has stolen — a more pressing matter than the bounty itself. So it's inevitable that when guns are drawn, blood will flow and men will die . . .

Books by Tyler Hatch
in the Linford Western Library:

A LAND TO DIE FOR
BUCKSKIN GIRL
DEATHWATCH TRAIL
LONG SHOT
VIGILANTE MARSHAL
FIVE GRAVES WEST
BIG BAD RIVER
CHEYENNE GALLOWS
DEAD WHERE YOU STAND!
DURANGO GUNHAWK
KNIFE EDGE
WILDE COUNTRY
WILDCATS
RAWHIDE RANSOM
BRAZOS FUGITIVE

TYLER HATCH

DEAD-END TRAIL

Complete and Unabridged

LINFORD
Leicester

First published in Great Britain in 2010 by
Robert Hale Limited
London

First Linford Edition
published 2012
by arrangement with
Robert Hale Limited
London

British Library CIP Data

Hatch, Tyler.
    Dead end trail.- -(Linford western library)
    1. Bounty hunters- -Fiction.
    2. Western stories.
    3. Large type books.
    I. Title II. Series
    823.9′2–dc23

    ISBN 978–1–4448–1059–2

Published by
F. A. Thorpe (Publishing)
Anstey, Leicestershire

Set by Words & Graphics Ltd.
Anstey, Leicestershire
Printed and bound in Great Britain by
T. J. International Ltd., Padstow, Cornwall

1

Dead-End

A dead man in need of a haircut.

That was what Chet Rand thought as he sat the big roan and looked down at the sprawled body of the man he had just killed in this dead-end canyon.

He had been tracking Feeney for two weeks, wondering what he really looked like — the blurred, hand-drawn illustrations on the Wanted dodgers were not much to go by.

Well, now he knew — a dead man in need of a haircut. A shave, too, going by the dirt-clogged stubble fringing the slack jaw: at least a week's growth. He must've been on the run almost constantly since the stage hold-up. The clothes, under the bloodstains, looked grimy, though. Maybe he hadn't been long on personal cleanliness — not that it mattered a cigarette paper in hell now.

Rand sat there, looking at the body; they had traded no more than a dozen shots after he had cornered Feeney in here. There had been lots of ricochets but Rand was certain he had hit Feeney twice in the chest. Square on.

So why was there that large spread of drying blood on the back of the grimy shirt, between the shoulders?

Stomach tightening, he dismounted, still holding the hot rifle, squatted warily. An old caution made him scan the rimrock which seemed to move across the sky as grey-tinged clouds scudded above. No one up there.

He examined the wound, that tightness in his belly suddenly iron-hard: it wasn't the jagged, slashed cut he expected to find, left by some berserk ricochet — but hard luck for Feeney, whatever had made the wound.

It was a clean bullet hole, round, edged with blood that no longer oozed. The semi-congealed blood surrounding

2

the wound had a thin, dulling skin on it.

Funny! It was only minutes since the shoot-out had ended. This bullet hole looked to be a good deal older than that. *What the hell!*

He turned Feeney over: dead as last week's rabbit stew. And two clean bullet holes in the chest!

But hardly any blood: Feeney must have been already dead when those slugs hit him over the heart.

He felt sweat trickle down his face, and, still squatting, backed into the rocks, once again scanning the rimrock. Then who the hell had been shooting back at him?

He watched till his eyes watered but there was no movement up there. If there had been another gunman — how or why he couldn't begin to explain — he was long gone. Or hiding, maybe . . . waiting?

For what? He'd been an easy target for ten minutes. No. If there was someone up there who'd put that slug into Feeney's back, he was gone by now.

The other thing was, a shot like that would have snapped Feeney's spine, killed him instantly.

Yet he had traded lead with Rand for at least ten minutes.

Someone had traded lead with him.

Rising slowly, rifle at the ready now, he stepped around the low rocks behind Feeney's body and found the man's horse.

It was lying on its side, its throat cut, the great pool of blood under its head congealed where it hadn't soaked into the earth. The carcass was cold, stiffening.

The saddle-bags were empty, the warbag, too.

If Feeney had still been carrying the loot from the hold-up, it had been stolen a second time — by his killer.

* * *

Sheriff Brock Powers jammed his thumbs behind his gunbelt as he

4

straightened from examining Feeney's body, draped over Rand's packhorse at the edge of the boardwalk.

A small crowd had gathered, following Rand down Springer Street as he made his way to the front of the law office. They stirred now as Powers looked bleakly at Rand and said,

'Backshot.'

'Not by me, Sheriff. I tracked Feeney to that dead-end canyon and while I was doing it I heard a shot. I thought Feeney had spotted me, but I never heard any bullet. I got into the canyon not long after and he was holed-up between two rocks, his rifle barrel covering the entrance. I hit the ground, snatching my own rifle, and we shot it out for a few minutes, no more than a dozen shots between us. I hit him twice in the chest and figured that was it. When I went to look I saw he'd been backshot, too.'

'No ricochet made that wound!' broke in the lawman, his voice hard-edged, his eyes narrowed. He was solidly built, a six-footer, late forties, horse-faced with a round jaw that jutted belligerently now. His stare was hard, cold and challenging.

His announcement brought further murmurings from the crowd.

'Hell! Feeney weren't all that bad!'

'He din' have to be shot in the back!'

'Judas priest! The dodgers never said anythin' about bringin' him in *dead*!'

Rand felt his face burning and he rounded on the crowd. 'Dammit! I didn't backshoot him!'

That caused a lot of shouting and a few shaken fists.

'The hell's wrong with you people? I never backshot him! But, in any case, he was a wanted outlaw with a bounty on his head and he was willing to fight to stay free.'

'So that's it!' cut in Powers. 'You're after the bounty!'

Rand felt the hard glares and held the lawman's gaze. 'I'm from Rattle Creek, Colorado. I had a small horse ranch there and a forest fire wiped me out. I need to rebuild and restock. I can catch and break mustangs, but I have to have money to build a house again and barns, fences and so on. I need a thousand dollars at least and I don't have it.'

Sheriff Powers nodded slowly. 'And the reward on Feeney is eleven hundred bucks.'

Rand nodded.

'You got a name?' Rand told him and Powers pursed his lips. 'Know of a few bounty hunters but can't say I've heard of you.'

'I'm not a bounty hunter. Dammit, I told you I'm a horse-rancher. I just came after Feeney when I saw a dodger on him.' Rand broke off, looking strangely at Powers. 'I didn't have to work very hard to learn this general neck of the woods was Feeney's stamping-ground, either, Sheriff.'

He let it hang and Powers' long face clouded. Then he straightened, dropping a hand to his gun butt.

'Climb on down, you son of a bitch! I

got about three hundred other things to do besides look for Boyd Feeney, a man who's been in some trouble hereabouts over the years, gettin' in a lotta folks' hair, but he never hurt no one while doin' it! They nicknamed him 'Gentle' Feeney — some even called him 'Feeble' Feeney.'

Rand dismounted slowly, seeing the lawman was mighty agitated. 'Then how come someone slapped over a thousand dollars reward on him if he was such small time?'

'Ah, that was the stage company put that up. They was shipping twelve thousand dollars on the quiet in the strongbox. No one was s'posed to know it held any more than the usual couple hundred, but that money was needed fast by a construction company workin' on the irrigation deal at Eagle Nest Lake. Feeney just struck it lucky, musta thought all his birthdays'd come at once.'

The crowd chuckled and had a few remarks to make.

Rand said, 'Would've thought that'd make you burn the candle at both ends, looking for him.'

'You got a mouth on you, feller! You keep flappin' it and you'll find it full of my gun barrel!' Powers thrust his big head close to Rand, who stood as tall as the lawman, eye-to-eye. 'We searched plenty for Feeney, but it's his stompin' ground out there in the Spare Ribs. He could run rings around any damn army troop, let alone a ragtag posse of townsmen.' He glanced at the stiff-faced crowd; some of the men had been in that posse. Powers gave a fleeting grin. 'But they was all triers, busted a gut on the job.'

They liked that better.

'And li'l ol' me comes along, tracks him down without raising a sweat hardly; I bring him in and lay him out on your doorstep. No wonder you're riled, Sheriff.'

Powers' eyes were mere slits now, slits in armour plate. He spoke slowly. 'You know what I think happened? I think you come up on Feeney and caught him with his pants down. You took the chance and put that bullet in his back — '

'Judas priest, how many times've I gotta — '

Powers continued as if Rand hadn't spoken. 'Well, no one likes a back-shooter, whether he nails an outlaw or anyone else. So you figured out this story you been pushin' at me and these fellers. You put a couple bullets into Feeney's chest, fired a few more at the rocks so's they'd leave streaks like ricochets, then come on in, talkin' about the gun battle you had in a dead-end canyon, all sassy 'n' ready to collect the bounty.'

Rand's insides were knotted like a greenhorn's bridle now. 'I'm beginning to think Feeney was a friend of yours, Sheriff.'

'OK! That's it! You're spendin' some time in my cells, mister!' Some of the crowd almost cheered, most of them at least nodded, going along with the sheriff. 'Personally, I got no time for any kinda backshooter, whether his target's a wanted man or not.'

Rand gritted his teeth. He was under the sheriff's gun, a hostile crowd behind him. He couldn't believe it: he'd brought in a wanted man with a reasonably sized bounty, on his head, and he was the villain!

'Look, Sheriff, I'll tell you what I think happened — '

'Tell it through the bars. Now come on in.'

Some of the crowd wanted to hear Rand's explanation and Powers scowled, finally nodded. 'Make it quick then! But I tell you now it ain't gonna make any difference.'

'I believe it. Like I said, I heard a gunshot about twenty minutes before I reached the canyon. I figure someone was up on the rimrock, waiting for Feeney, who was likely watching for me when he should've been watching his own back. I had a notion he knew I was getting close. He was likely crouching by the rock where I found him and whoever was up on the rim had a great target, all ready and waiting.' Rand spread his hands. 'He nailed Feeney, climbed down, killed Feeney's mount and searched his saddle-bags and warbag. Then I arrived. The killer jammed Feeney's body between those two rocks, poked his rifle under his arm and started pot-shotting at me. I shot back, naturally, and put a couple into Feeney's chest. The killer lit out with whatever he'd found in Feeney's gear while I was busy looking at the dead man.'

Powers scoffed, spat to one side. 'You got a mighty wild imagination, friend.'

'Aw, I dunno, Brock,' one of the townsmen in the front of the crowd said. 'It — it just coulda happened that way.'

A couple of others agreed and even the sheriff heaved a sigh and allowed, 'Well. Yeah, OK, it's possible. But I like it better this sonuver killed Feeney and figured out his story, then rode in here to collect the bounty.'

The majority of the crowd liked that version, too, and Powers grinned tightly, jerking his gun barrel.

'There's one other thing, Rand. *Two*. First, what happened to the money Feeney stole? And, second, if your story's gospel, it means someone else nailed Feeney, so you ain't eligible for the bounty at all!'

Brock Powers grinned, showing his teeth.

'Now hand over your Colt and get inside. Someone get Feeney down to the undertaker's. An' tell Doc Swanson I want a full account of them bullet wounds. Now, Mr Rand, if you're ready? Your cell awaits, you backshootin' son of a bitch!'

2

Columbine Jail

There was a drunk in the cell next to Rand's.

He was lying on the bunk and through the bars that separated the cells, Rand could see a straggly mop of iron-grey hair, a big nose that seemed to tremble as he snored and part of a scrawny neck that showed grime in saggy wrinkles even from this distance and in the poor light. His clothes seemed to be cast-offs from people of different sizes, his boots were dirty and run-over, but the soles were intact.

His snores rattled the bars.

'Hey! *Hey!* Old-timer. Roll over and quit sawing wood, will you?'

He was surprised to see one bleary eye pop open. Prune lips moved outwards and blew until the hair dragging across the drunk's face lifted. He ran a tongue around his lips and started to struggle up on to an elbow, squinting at Rand with pale-blue eyes. 'Hah! Go' some compn'y, have I? Welcome to my humble abode, sir. You may call me 'The Duke' or just 'Duke' — as in Duke of Columbine, New Mexico Territory.'

Rand smiled crookedly. 'Does Columbine know?'

The old man looked surprised, then displayed a set of gums with gapped and worn teeth showing. 'Hah! That is the first time that question has been posed to me, suh. I'm sure this town knows me, but perhaps not in any . . . ducal sense. Oh-oh!'

Suddenly the stick-thin legs in the tattered trousers swung over the side of the bunk and the old face looked startled, cheeks blowing out as a bony, trembling hand lifted quickly to the old mouth.

Too late.

Rand grimaced and turned away as

the old man retched and hawked and finally vomited. He moved to the far corner of his own cell to get away from the sour stench while The Duke made enough noise to stir the inhabitants of Boot Hill across town.

The racket had been enough to bring Brock Powers charging in from his office. He skidded to a halt outside the other cell.

'You stinkin' old polecat! Look at the mess you've made! Jeeeeesus! I told you last time you spewed in my cells I'd ram your head through the wall. And, by God, I'll do it!'

He fumbled his keys and slammed the door back even as the oldster, shaken by his efforts, struggled to get off the bunk. There was nowhere to run, of course, and Powers' big left hand caught the old material of the grey shirt and dragged the bag of bones upright, shaking him.

'I — told — you!'

The sheriff emphasized each word with slaps from his right hand, back and forth, then played a rapid tattoo across the wrinkled cheeks, rocking the man's head so that his hair flew wild.

'Cut it out!'

Powers paused, turned his bleak gaze towards Rand who was at the dividing bars now.

'You — shut — up!' Powers shook The Duke again and batted him once more across the face.

'Big, brave lawman! Poor bastard can't even fight back. You want to try me?'

Powers smiled thinly, that savage stare intensifying if anything. 'When I'm ready, Rand. When — I'm — ready.'

On each word he hit the old man again, then drove a blow into his midriff. The Duke collapsed, groaning and retching, writhing in pain. But Brock Powers gave him no rest. He fisted up some more of the collarless shirt and heaved the oldster to his feet, steadying him as he sagged and swayed.

He dragged him out of the cell and started down the passage towards the front office.

'Leave him be, goddamn you!'

'Be patient, Rand. I'll get around to you. Meantime, just *shut up*!'

Rand was at the front cell door now, knuckles white where his hands gripped the bars. He had to press his face hard against the iron so he could see down the passage. The sheriff dragged the stumbling oldster through the door leading to the front office.

What kind of a man could beat up on an oldster like that? He wasn't a man at all! He was a bullying, sadistic son of a bitch!

Minutes later Rand rose from the bunk and pushed his face hard against the bars again.

Powers was shoving The Duke down the passage towards the fouled cell. The oldster was trying to carry a pail of soapy water and had a long-handled mop tucked under one arm.

The sheriff barely glanced at Rand as he sent him stumbling into the cell, water slopping.

'Now, sudsy-mudgee it out, you

stinkin' old skunk! An' I mean the walls, too, the bunk legs, and specially the floor. They all better be clean enough to eat a meal off when I come back or I'll use you as a mop! Now — get — to it!'

The Duke staggered, got his balance and plunged his mop into the soapy water. He twisted it expertly before applying it to the floor and Rand knew it wasn't the first time he had done this chore.

Powers produced a cheroot and lit up. He came and stood outside Rand's cell. 'Think I'm a bastard, huh?'

'That's only one of the things I think about you, Powers.'

The sheriff smiled thinly. 'You're a bushy-tailed cougar, ain't you? But you're kinda forgettin' where you are, feller — and who I am.'

'I haven't forgot a thing.'

Powers' face straightened. He dragged on the cheroot and blew smoke. 'Faster, you old coot!' he shouted at The Duke, then gave Rand his attention again. 'Don't think you'll be outta here any time soon, Rand. I've got a lot to investigate about you. Could take me a couple weeks, mebbe more. And if it don't satisfy me, why — I might have to drag you up before our Judge Stanton. You know about him? Aw, got bad ulcers and a mean disposition that a mule'd envy. I go and interrupt his dinner or his mornin' chat with his cronies an' he'll bust a blood vessel. He might give me a little tongue-lashin', but when I bring you up before him, *you*'ll be the one he blames. He's sent more'n one man to the chain gang or rock pile on the strength of such a thing.'

'You're just plain miserable, Powers.'

The sheriff didn't like that but he forced a crooked grin. 'Well, I'm in a position to make you miserable, anyway. I'll let you think about that.' He stepped into the cell where the oldster was sweating over his mop now and cuffed him across one ear. 'Do it good, damn you! You've had enough practice.'

He winked at Rand and drew on his

cheroot as he sauntered off down the passage. Rand heard the door close after him.

'You OK?'

The oldster dabbed some blood away from his nostrils, which looked like mouseholes, they were so big, and spat. 'Yeah. That wasn't too bad. He's busted me up worse.'

'He's a mean bastard.'

'Sure. But ain't nothin' anyone can do about it.'

'How far off is election?'

The Duke of Columbine made a strange sound that took Rand a minute or so to identify as bitter laughter way back in the old throat.

'Too far for folk to remember his meanness when it comes time to mark the ballot papers. See, he runs this town, keeps it quiet for the regular folk. An' turns his back when prices go through the roof if a trail herd hits town. That's what they want, and they're in the majority. They know he won't bother *them*, unless they're stupid enough to break the law. Sorry for this mess, mister.'

Rand told him his name as he watched the old man swamp out the cell. 'What're you in for?'

'Aw, just sleeping away the hours. 'Course I was kinda sorta drunk, too, but you might've noticed we've had some rain. So Powers threw me in here for three-four days.'

Rand looked puzzled and The Duke grinned showing his tough old gums again.

'Yeah. It keeps me dry, more ways than one, while I'm in the cells. Caught pneumonia once, nearly died, but Doc Swanson pulled me through. His infirmary was full of kids with measles and he didn't know how he could fit me in. So he made Powers give me a cell all to myself — see that one in the corner? Warm and dry, best in the house . . . '

Rand looked incredulous. 'And he lets you come in outta the rain, but still beats the hell out of you?'

The old man shrugged his bony

shoulders. 'I can't pay him anything. If I gotta take a coupla punches to stay out of our inclement weather — well, I can stand it.'

Rand shook his head slowly. 'You're both loco. And how come you talk like you do?' As The Duke raised eyebrows he added, 'Like a deadbeat drunk sometimes, then you mix in a few words in a way I wouldn't figure you'd know about.'

The gums gleamed again briefly. 'B'lieve it or not, suh, I walked the boards once upon a time. The boards . . . ? *The stage,* my friend. Not for long. The temptation of those lovely bare-limbed young ladies changing costumes between scenes was just too much for me. Unfortunately, I liked them young and . . . inexperienced, if you know what I mean. It became prudent for me to stay away from such places — right away, and . . . well, take it from me, young feller, a bottle is no substitute for kitten-soft white arms clinging around your neck tight enough to cut off your air.'

Rand grinned despite himself. 'You old rogue.'

'Ah, I have lots of memories to keep me company . . . ' Those pale-blue eyes took on a sudden nostalgic look. 'Duke Mandrell, I was once known as, among the royalty of a company that butchered the Bard in the backblocks. The yokels loved it, and we loved them back — their womenfolk, anyway. Ah, such memories . . . '

'I don't hear that mop a'swampin'!' called the sheriff from his office. 'If I gotta come in there . . . '

The Duke got working again in a hurry. As he passed close to the bars he asked, 'An' what transgression, my friend, are you incarcerated for? If I may ask . . . ?'

'I tracked down and killed a man named Feeney and brought the body in so I could collect the bounty. But Powers seems kinda reluctant to pay me.'

The oldster stopped swamping again,

looked sharply at Rand. 'Would that be Boyd Feeney?' Rand nodded and the old prune lips pursed. 'Bad luck, friend. The Feeneys are distant kin to the Powers.'

'Kin?' Rand was startled.

'Aye. Boyd would be the nephew of Brock's wife — now deceased. Strong on kin, them folk.'

Rand went and sat on his bunk. He blew out his lips.

'I guess I'll never see that bounty now.'

'You don't look like a bounty hunter.'

'How do they look? Fangs, and a gun in each hand?'

'Mmmm — see what you mean. Wouldn't be such a big bounty on Boyd if it weren't for the stageline. Feeney hurt their feelings, stealing that particular strongbox. They went to a deal of trouble to make sure it was all hush-hush, but someone must've let something slip.'

'Way I heard it, Feeney was just lucky.'

The mop stopped working again. The

pale eyes were serious. 'Well, here's a thought: Feeney wasn't much of an outlaw, piddling little crimes, more nuisance than anything else. He worked alone — but, for the first time, he had a pardner when he held up that stage.'

Rand frowned, stepped across to the bars. 'I looked into it pretty closely, Duke. I found no sign of a pardner.'

''Course not. He stayed out of sight. But there's one young lady was a passenger on that coach, only gal with three men. Feeney hit the stage at a ford while the horses were resting and passengers took a brush-ticket: gents to the right, lady to the left. While she was communing with Nature, she saw a masked man holding the getaway horses among the trees. Scared out of her wits, of course, but managed to stay quiet and get back on board. She kept mum.'

'Why didn't she mention it to Powers?'

The old mouth moved into a strange shape and then exposed the gums in that grin that, with a full set of teeth, must have sent many a young lady into a swoon years ago. 'I guess she had her reasons.'

'How come she told you?'

'Who said she did? But, you're right — she did tell me. I earn a drink or two by swampin' out the saloon now and again — showed her a few fancy dances that make the boys' eyes pop. Know 'em from my own stage experience. We're good friends.'

'She works at a saloon?'

He hesitated, then nodded. 'The Shotglass. A singer and dancer. I gave her the benefit of my past experience in exchange for whiskey.' He started to drift off into nostalgia again until Rand brought him back with sharp words.

'What did she say about Feeney — and his 'pard'?'

'Just what I told you. He was masked with a bandanna. She couldn't recognize him.'

'She still work at this saloon?'

'Aye. Name's Jackie Holt, sometimes called 'Ginger' because of her hair.' He looked slightly uncomfortable. 'I — hope you won't betray my trust, Young Rand, but you read like a decent fellow.'

Rand nodded a little absently. 'I won't say who told me unless I have to, Duke. See, Powers thinks I backshot Feeney. But I reckon there was another man in that canyon who knew Feeney had the loot. If I can find *him*, I might get some satisfaction out of Powers.'

'You're really hungry for that bounty, eh?' The Duke sounded a little disappointed but brightened when Rand told him why he needed the money. 'Well, first, of course, you have to get outta here,' the oldster pointed out smugly but unnecessarily.

But it wasn't really hard at all.

★ ★ ★

Brock Powers sauntered down late in the afternoon, a bunch of keys in his hand. He glanced into The Duke's cell

28

where the oldster was snoring on his bunk, one skinny leg in its ragged trousers dangling over the side.

'Still stinks,' the sheriff said, moving to Rand's cell, working a key into the lock.

Rand sat up quickly on the bunk, swung his legs over the side, looking puzzled. The sheriff pushed the door open and jerked his head. He dropped his right hand to the butt of his holstered Colt as Rand picked up his hat and set it on his head, eyes on the lawman all the time.

'Where?'

'You want me to lock the door again?'

Rand stepped out past the lawman and turned quickly to face him. Powers looked mildly amused, left the door open and pointed down the passage.

In the front office sat a man in a frock-coat that showed signs of age but some care in the creases in the sleeves and the way the collar had been ironed flat and batwinged. His shirt had seen a lot of wear, but had been neatly repaired where necessary. The striped brown trousers were old, but the half-boots gleamed with neatsfoot oil.

The man himself was in his fifties, wore a derby hat above a lined face with weary eyes and a mouth that hadn't smiled in a long time. He yawned, making no effort to cover his mouth.

'Doc Swanson,' Powers said briefly, going around his desk and dropping into his chair.

Rand didn't see any spare chairs so stood between the sheriff's desk and the doctor.

'Tell him, Doc.'

The medico had been holding an envelope in his hand. He now lifted it and spilled three misshapen pieces of lead on to the desk.

'You're a man who can recognize bullets dug out of a body, I suspect, bounty hunter.' There was disapproval in the doctor's voice, although he kept his face expressionless.

'I don't make a habit of bounty

hunting, Doc.' Rand was annoyed that he felt he had to defend himself. 'First time, matter of fact.'

His words had no effect whatsoever on Doctor Swanson. He poked at the hunks of lead, separated them with a pencil taken from Powers' side of the desk, two on one side, the other, slightly larger, by itself.

He poked at the pair. 'I have removed many bullets from bodies, both living and dead, Mr Rand. I have made a hobby of judging the calibre. In addition, I studied the appropriate books and I'm the nearest thing to an expert in ballistics you'll find this side of San Francisco. These two, of course, are forty-five calibre. What does your rifle shoot?'

Rand nodded to the twin pieces of lead. 'That's my calibre. Bought the rifle by mail order from the Winchester factory. They're chambering a new line of rifles in .45 Colt, and it suits me because my six-gun takes the same calibre.'

Powers watched with narrowed stare.

'What every good bounty hunter would want, huh? Only need to carry one size cartridge.'

'That seems prudent,' opined the doctor, sounding neither approving nor critical — or very much interested. He poked at the slightly larger piece of misshapen lead. 'This is .56 calibre, though I might've expected .44/.40, that used by most Winchester rifles, in country where the target may be anything from a bobcat to a bear.' The old eyes took on a little expression now as he set his gaze on Rand's face. 'But this is from a Sharps, or even an old Spencer carbine. I dug it out of Boyd Feeney's back. It shattered his spine so he would've died instantly.'

Rand swung his gaze to the sheriff. 'So there was someone else up there on that rimrock after all.'

Powers scowled as he nodded. 'Seems so. You arrived before he could get away, and he set Feeney up between a couple of rocks to hold him, poked

Boyd's rifle through and started shooting to make you think Feeney was still alive. Then took off while you thought you were exchanging shots with Feeney.'

Rand nodded, mouth a little tight. 'I fell for it — and I shot Feeney twice in the chest.'

'But he was already dead!' Powers said, sitting up straighter and then leaning forward across his desk. 'So, that means that because you didn't kill him . . . ' he paused to smile crookedly now, taking pleasure in pointing it out, 'you can't claim the bounty.'

Rand swore silently, face hard now. 'You mean the backshooter could?'

The medic made a wide gesture with his long-fingered hands. 'A fine point in law, I think. But a lawman would have a good deal of influence in the final say, I believe.'

Rand sighed. 'OK. Well, at least you can't hold me for murder.'

'No.' Even with that one short word, Powers sounded disappointed. 'You can leave. Just as fast as you can saddle your horse. Leave all the way, Rand!'

'Getting dark outside, Brock,' Doc Swanson pointed out. 'You could let him stay overnight, couldn't you?'

'Aah — I guess so,' Powers growled, giving Rand that brittle stare. 'Be gone by mid-morning, or I'll throw you back in the cells.'

Powers opened a cupboard, taking out Rand's gunbelt and rifle, placing them on the end of his desk. 'Put it on outside, and keep the gun in its holster.'

Rand nodded, picked up his money and clasp knife, then his guns. 'Obliged, Doc.'

Swanson nodded. He rose slowly to his feet stifling another yawn. 'I'll walk some of the way with you.'

Rand didn't bother saying goodbye to Powers.

Outside, buckling on his gunrig, Rand asked, 'You take a look at The Duke while you were there, Doc?'

'Yes. You were sleeping at the time. He's not hurt badly. Tough old feller.'

'Why the hell does Powers do it? I mean, Duke says he'll let him have a cell when it's raining or cold and so on. Then he beats the hell out of him.'

For the first time Doc Swanson smiled, the westering sun's slanting rays outlining the creases around his mouth. 'Interesting case, our sheriff — very interesting.'

'That's one way of putting it.'

'I turn off here. Good night, Mr Rand.'

''Night, Doc, and thanks.' Rand started across the street, making for the The Shotglass saloon.

3

Ginger

The drinkers made it plain that Rand wasn't popular. The barkeep half-filled his beer glass with a deep collar of froth that prompted Rand to ask, as the man deliberately slopped the drink when setting it on the counter.

'Got a neckerchief to go with that collar?'

'One nickel,' the man growled. He had a face that had been beaten many times. He placed one ham fist palm-up on the counter. 'You want it or don't you?'

'Fill it up with beer, then I'll want it.'

The 'keep moved his scarred lips and showed big teeth. 'I was kinda hopin' you'd be hard-nosed about it.'

'I kinda thought you would be.'

'Well?' A challenge. Waiting — impatient.

Rand pursed his lips, sighed. 'OK.'

Then he brought his rifle up and slammed the butt between the barkeep's eyes. The man was rammed backwards, crashed into the shelf of bottles and joined them on the floor as they toppled, some breaking.

Rand wheeled, levering a shell into the rifle's breech, holding the weapon down close to his hip, finger on the trigger as he swept the muzzle slowly around the suddenly silent, tensed drinkers. A few men leapt to their feet.

'I didn't backshoot Feeney. Wrong calibre of bullet broke his spine — from above. Ask Doc Swanson. You'll likely be glad to know I can't claim the bounty, either.' That got a couple of cheers and started some murmuring. 'I came in for a drink, but I reckon I'll settle for a cup of coffee in the diner. Night, gents.'

He backed towards the door on the rear wall. No one tried to stop him. Then he saw a young girl with ginger hair standing on a small platform decorated with worn old ribbons and even a few sagging sprigs of holly from last Christmas. There were two other bar girls with her, but they looked much more used and had bored expressions and tight, go-to-hell mouths. The platform was used as a kind of stage for the saloon's resident entertainers: a little singing and crude dancing, an occasional strip; the real 'entertainment' that most customers required of the painted women was carried on in more private places. The form it took was up to them, as was the price: whatever the traffic would bear, as long as they gave the agreed percentage to the saloon owner. The ginger-haired girl was watching Rand and started to smile slightly, some kind of interest showing on her babyish face.

'A real live curly-wolf,' she said, slightly mocking.

'You Jackie Holt?' he asked.

Surprised, she nodded automatically and he walked closer. 'You got a room where we can talk?'

'My room is not usually used for — talking.'

He smiled. 'Might not be a helluva lot of talking going on for a spell.' He crooked an arm and offered it to her. 'But — after — we could chat.'

The drinkers seemed to hold their breath as the girl gave him an open appraisal. She was small in stature but adequately endowed in places where it mattered; she showed a good deal of her charms with her bare shoulders and low-cut bodice. Rand watched her calculating eyes, contrasting with her baby-faced looks. She ran a tongue quickly over the pouty, painted lips. 'Mmmmmm . . . ' she murmured thoughtfully. Then she smiled coquettishly and took a step towards him, obviously interested, as the door behind Rand crashed open. The edge caught him in the back, knocked him staggering.

He didn't have to be told that the two men who entered were the saloon's bouncers. Both had short wooden clubs, and came at him fast, swinging. The girl gave a small cry, a hand going to her face as Rand ducked the first club but felt it skid off his shoulder, numbing his neck and arm. He swung the rifle one-handed and the heavy barrel slammed across the side of the man's head. He staggered and stumbled two yards until he hit the wall and fell to his knees, gagging and bleeding.

Rand dodged the second man, brought up the butt in a tight arc that knocked him back across a table, his jaw and mouth all bloody. Then, as he looked around at the gawking crowd, the barkeep, bloody-faced and raging, came charging at him with a broken bottle raised, ready to do some butchering.

Rand dropped to one knee, shoved the rifle between the man's legs. The 'keep yelled, lurched, put out his hands as he fell. The already broken bottle shattered and sliced his flesh, a little finger hanging by a shred. He howled and lost all interest in Rand or anything else except his new wound, now spurting blood.

'Reckon that's about enough, Rand!'

Rand turned swiftly. Brock Powers stood there with a cocked six-gun, looking as if he would like to use it. 'Lose the rifle.'

Rand slid the Winchester on to a nearby table, recently abandoned by a couple of drinkers who figured they were too close to the brawl. 'All right. Who started it?'

Many voices spoke at once and several fingers pointed at Rand, bringing a crooked grin to Powers' face.

'Now, wonder why I even had to ask? You're a damn troublemaker, mister.'

'Wouldn't've been any trouble if you'd put out the word I didn't backshoot Feeney. Christ, he seems to've been some kind of hero to this damn town, instead of the outlaw described on the Wanted dodgers.'

'Feeney wasn't so bad.' Then Powers

looked at the crowd and nodded, told them it was true, Doc Swanson had cleared Rand of killing Feeney.

Rand was surprised the sheriff had spoken out so readily and honestly, was even more surprised when Powers said, 'You'd've done better to quit town like I told you. Where you want to spend the night? I can accommodate you free of charge next to The Duke . . . '

Rand stared and then swung his gaze to the ginger-haired girl.

'Already decided on a room. If I can have some nice company.' He arched his eyebrows at the girl who stared back soberly.

Then, as he shrugged, she suddenly asked, 'You got money?'

'Some. If you don't charge too much.'

'Maybe I'll make a special rate for you.'

The sheriff scowled and some of the drinkers nudged each other. 'You still be gone by mid-mornin', Rand!'

'Sure. If I can crawl aboard my hoss.'

He offered his arm again to the

smiling girl and she turned him towards the stairs leading to the upper floor.

*   *   *

Between deep, satisfied breaths as she watched Rand buckle his trouser belt, Ginger said, 'I like a man who can take care of himself, and still give a woman . . . pleasure.'

'I noticed,' he allowed, getting into his shirt. He sat on the edge of the bed where she lay with only a crumpled sheet covering her. He buttoned up his sleeves and shirt front, pulled on his boots. 'I hear you were the only woman on that stage that Feeney robbed.'

Her flushed and sweat-sheened face straightened and something clouded in her eyes. 'So . . . ?'

'You must've heard about the trouble I had — being blamed for shooting Feeney in the back.' She nodded warily, still fighting to get her breathing back to normal. 'There was a whisper going around that he might've had a pard to hold the getaway mounts in that hold-up.'

'I hadn't heard that.'

He smiled and shook a finger under her nose. Her eyes blazed and she sat up abruptly, snatching the sheet and holding it slantwise across her breasts — a little late in the piece for modesty.

'Feeney was a loner.'

'So everyone says — but this time he had help. You ask me, he knew damn well that strongbox held a slew of money this time, and he wanted to make sure he got away in a hurry. So he had his pard standing by with the mounts all ready to go. He was seen, but he was masked and wasn't recognized.'

Eyes narrowed, mouth taut, she said nothing. Her bosom heaved, but no longer with the after-effects of passion: she was tensing up mighty fast. Then, in a voice not much louder than a whisper, she said, 'I only told one person about that! And you were in the cell next to him! Damn that old man!'

Then she frowned. 'But why would he tell you? You know him from somewhere?'

Rand shook his head. 'Powers beat on him and I had a few words to say. Didn't stop the beating but The Duke seemed grateful for me trying.'

'That sheriff! Miserable son of a bitch! They say his father was a drunk and beat him every day of his life. And now he's gettin' his own back, thinks every old drunk and deadbeat is like his father . . . ' The anger still showed on her face, then alarm started to replace it. Her small hands fisted up the crumpled sheets. 'You — you haven't told anyone?'

He shook his head again. 'Wondered if there was any more you had to add — and why you told old Duke at all.'

'Oh, he — he takes an interest in me, teaches me some French dancing for my act downstairs.' She winked. 'Got me a lot more customers. I do a solo cancan. You know that dance?'

'I've heard tell.'

45

'You can get that gleam outta your eye! I seen your roll and you don't have enough for a private performance!'

'Too bad. Can you tell me anything else? I'd sure like to catch up with Feeney's pard.'

'You think he shot Feeney in the back?'

'Well, one of 'em must've had the loot. Or mebbe Feeney's pard got greedy, just as I happened along to that canyon. Some mighty fast thinking on his part, setting things up the way he did. Thought I was shooting it out — but it was with a dead man.'

'Ye-es, he — ' The girl caught herself and started to cough, an obvious false effort. But she wiped her mouth with the edge of the sheet and studied Rand thoughtfully for a long minutee. Then she said, quite breathlessly, 'I was terrified to move in the bushes. I froze. Then Feeney came running back dragging the strong box, and he said, 'Gimme a hand to tie it on behind my saddle, Riley, and let's vamoose!' '

'Riley? Could be first or last name.'

She was breathing fast now and he frowned at the expression on her face. He couldn't make it out. Her eyes seemed to be suddenly glistening and her hands mangled the sheet as her teeth tugged at her lower lip.

Then he had a notion of what she was thinking. 'Was it — did you think you knew who it was when Feeney called him by name?'

She snapped her head up. 'No! Of course not! I-I was scared because my foot slipped and made a crackling sound in some dead leaves. They both looked towards where I was crouched and . . . I feel sick now, just remembering.' She tossed her ginger hair and he could see her making an effort to regain full control. 'I was scared they'd kill me if they found me there.' She gave a quick, on-off smile. 'But they didn't. *Riley* — that's what Boyd Feeney called the man holding the horses. They started to argue about which horse the box was tied to but Feeney still had his gun in his hand and called the tune. They slung it behind his saddle and rode off.'

'Together? Or did they separate?'

Her frown came back as she thought about it. 'They went in opposite directions, but on my way back to the stage — Feeney had made the driver unhitch the team and then run them off — I saw the one called Riley swinging around in a long arc that would eventually bring him up behind Feeney.'

Rand nodded. 'Didn't trust Feeney with the loot. Feeney might've lost him and it took Riley a week or so to catch up with him — in that dead-end canyon where I cornered him.'

'You — you're going after this Riley now?'

He looked at her sharply. 'Would, if I knew where to look. You didn't tell Powers this?' She shook her head quickly, lips compressed. 'How come?'

'Don't like him. He — hurts me when he visits. The other girls complain, too. Wouldn't throw a cup of cold coffee on him if he was on fire.'

It could well be true, Rand allowed, but there seemed to be something else that sounded not quite right with the way she told her story . . . something he couldn't figure.

*   *   *

He was saddling his mount in the livery stall next morning about eleven when The Duke dragged himself down the aisle. One eye was blackened and closed. His mouth was swollen and cut with a rim of dried blood outlining the lips. He limped and favoured his midriff, a hand pressed into the arch beneath his ribs.

'Howdy.'

'Powers beat up on you again?' Rand gritted but the oldster waved it aside, showing some annoyance at the question. 'Why the hell does he do it . . . and you let him?'

'Nothin' to git excited about. He give me two bits to get some grub.' He winked his good eye and ran a tongue over swollen parched lips. 'Or whatever two bits'll buy. Figured I'd find you here about this time.'

Tightening the cinch strap Rand nodded. 'Don't want any more trouble with Powers. The man's plumb loco. Mebbe I'll have a word with him before I go — on your behalf.'

Duke held up a hand and shook his head, long, greasy strands of grey hair flopping across his forehead.

'Don't. 'Tain't worth it. He can make a heap of trouble for you. See Ginger?' He flicked his eyebrows and leered so that Rand couldn't help smiling. He cackled. 'Show you a good time, did she? Yeah, every cowhand races to get into town on pay day and tries to be first in line. Wish I was twenty years younger.'

As the oldster's memory began to stir, Rand told him, 'She worked out you had to be the one to tell me she'd seen Feeney's pard. Says Feeney called him 'Riley'.'

The Duke stiffened. 'That so. Riley, eh?'

'That seems to've gotten your interest.'

'Yeah. Well, there's an outlaw lives in the Cherokee Strip across the line, name of Riley Duggan. Wouldn't be the first hold-up he's been mixed up in, though he mostly sticks to banks. Got a gang. Still, I wonder . . .'

'You think he could be the one?' The oldster nodded slightly, obviously thinking hard. 'Know where I can find him? I mean, the Cherokee Strip's a big place.'

'And crawlin' with murderin' hard-cases. You set on goin' in there?'

'If there's a chance I can find this Duggan.'

'Well, I can give you a rough idea — but only rough, mind. Be damn dangerous.'

'Tell me all you can, old-timer. I'm going after him.'

Duke squinted. 'Powers still won't authorize that bounty. Says you never killed Feeney, just brought in a dead man.'

Rand looked at him soberly as he tied on his warbag.

'If Riley's got the loot, the stage company'll pay a reward for that. Likely more than the one on Feeney.'

Duke looked thoughtful. 'Or — if Riley has the loot,' he said slowly, 'and you can take it away from him, you won't really need a reward — if you know what I mean.'

'Funny you should say that,' Rand replied without turning from his chore. 'It had crossed my mind.'

The old man stared, then shook his head.

'Nah. You wouldn't keep it. Not your style.'

Now Rand looked at the oldster squarely.

'I guess I'm like most men, Duke — I can be tempted. But first I have to find Riley.'

'Make sure your gun's loaded and cocked when you do. He's mean and he's fast.'

4

Night Riders

He crossed from New Mexico into badman's territory just before sundown.

The country looked better than he had expected: green slopes, tree-clad hills, a few streams. But the brooding rock-scarred mountains reared against the blood-coloured sky with its streaks of red-gold clouds. He had been told they housed dozens, if not hundreds, of outlaws on the run, beyond the reach of even a federal warrant (though there were ways of getting around this and making the venture at least semi-legal).

'You watch out, Chet,' The Duke had warned him worriedly. 'Plenty of them fellers'll shoot first and talk later. Ain't no comeback for any crime known to man in there. You seem to have good eyes — *use* 'em — and your ears, too. Or you'll be buzzard meat.'

So Rand rode with his rifle loaded, and thumb on the hammer, butt resting against his left thigh, hat brim tugged down against the ruddy glare as his eyes swept the hills.

They were in deep shadow this side, black as any night he had ever seen, with the sun sinking behind them and making rugged cut-outs of the crests. But he was really more interested in his back trail.

Twice he had seen what could have been a small cloud of swirling dust back there during the afternoon. There had been a breeze blowing, too, so it was hard to decide whether it was a dust-devil whipped up by the breeze, or just drifting dust from two or three careless riders.

The sensible thing to do was accept it was the latter, and take all necessary precautions.

The first thing he did was rake the roan's flanks with his spurs and set the startled animal into a run. He had picked out the entrance to a gulch which he figured led into a canyon. He guided the horse towards this. The gulch opening was narrow and the roan skidded, hitting one edge, crumbling dirt and starting a small cascade of gravel.

Damn! That would be a fine signpost for anyone tracking him!

Couldn't be helped, and no sense in blaming the horse. He guided it through the twisting gulch, seeing gravel slopes giving way to steeper walls studded with rock and, eventually, a cliff with a couple of narrow ledges and a rock-studded face.

He smiled in grim satisfaction: the beginning of the canyon he had expected, going by the geologic formations, was right there and waiting. A mustang man made good use of such sign and thereby learned the hideaways of the wild horses, always guarded by the stallion leader on some high ground; it might be out of sight until he saw danger approaching, then there would be the shrill warning scream alerting the herd, followed quickly by the challenge. The horse would show itself, rise on to its hind legs, forelegs pawing the air as the teeth were bared and the piercing cry echoed from the rock walls.

But not this time. No wild stallion ready to take on the world, just the canyon opening out. A waterhole gleamed like a large pool of blood as the sky deepened in colour. Shadows like black knives slashed across the slopes and ledges and benches, carving them into geometric shapes.

He chose his campsite within min-utes, rode there and started setting up. ' It was at the base of a leaning flat rock with a row of boulders a few yards away. He built his fire close to the flat rock, not too big, just large enough to cook a meal and brew coffee. His rifle was right alongside the skillet and his eating utensils as he worked, facing the entrance which was now almost indiscernible as darkness flooded in on the tide of a fast-falling mountain night.

After his meal, cigarette between his lips as he worked, he spread his blankets between the fire and the boulders as a man will in the chill of night, even this late in the season in these parts. Heat would bounce off the flat wall behind the fire, down on to the bedroll, and bounce back again when it struck the row of boulders. It was a snug camp, set up by someone with wilderness savvy, apparently unconcerned about intruders. But there were some refinements.

As he let the fire die down to glowing coals, he humped his saddle-bags and spare clothes under the blankets in the rough shape of a human body, placed his hat at the top.

In the deep shadows he took a quick, unobtrusive turn of his lariat around the rumpled pile of clothes, ran it back between two boulders. Then he made an act of building up the fire a little, yawning, urinating and taking off his boots.

Still in shadow, he sat down beside the bed and lifted the blanket so as to slide under.

Except he dived the other way as he let the blanket fall, landing between two rocks and swiftly rolling behind one. After a minute or two of anxious groping, he found his rope and brought it in close against him, taking up any slack. He stretched out, just able to reach his rifle on the dark side of the bed, the side closest to him.

When he gripped the cold barrel, he pulled it in and cradled it in his arms. The magazine was full, an extra cartridge in the breech. He only had to cock the hammer and start shooting — if necessary.

Keyed up now, he couldn't even doze, but sat there, quietly swearing at the mosquitoes, afraid to slap at them in case it gave away his position. When he moved he did so as if an enemy might be within a few feet of him and could hear the rustle of his clothing or the involuntary grunt as he shifted his weight to prevent cramps. By this time his eyes had grown used to the darkness.

When he heard the first stones clunk together near the gulch entrance, he tensed. Someone was down there. A pale blur moved in odd motions, swinging in a short arc, rising, dropping down again, swinging once more, disappearing, then reappearing several feet closer to the camp.

It was too low for a man's pale hat; even too low to be a light-coloured shirt or jacket as a man stalked his camp . . .

He suddenly grinned. *A bandage!* A thick, white wadded bandage, like the sawbones had used to bind up the saloon barkeep's badly cut hand!

Well, Rand sure hadn't expected *him* to be one of the men following him. But he figured the man wouldn't come alone.

Just as the thought formed, he heard someone curse — several yards closer to the camp, startling him. He tugged gently on the rope and the wadded clothing beneath the blanket moved, as if a man was restlessly turning over in his sleep.

'Quiet!' a voice hissed over to the right.

Hell! Three of them!

'He's turnin' over, Jer! Could be awake!'

A hissed curse. 'He will be you don't shut up!'

Rand tensed, slowly and silently cocked the rifle hammer, easing himself down by inches until he was prone behind a V formed by two large rocks.

He drew bead on that moving bandaged hand, raised the barrel, followed its movements as well as he could.

Then one of them yelled and he was startled to find the other two much closer than he expected as they surged up the slope, pumping two shots into the bedroll.

'Shoot for his legs! Goddamnit, Milt!

I wish we'd left you behind!'

'You might've tried!' gasped an over-excited Milt, jumping up to stand beside the bedroll, kicking it. 'Get up, you son of a — *Judas!* It's a trap!'

Milt dropped instantly to one knee and might even have glimpsed Rand's head between the rocks as he triggered his rifle again, this time one-handed. The lead whined off the rock beside Rand's left shoulder and his own weapon spoke in a series of whiplash sounds that echoed through the canyon like a squad of troopers opening up.

Milt yelled and spun, staggered a couple of feet, then toppled back down the rise. The man running in from the right had his carbine butt braced into his hip, shooting very fast and very wild.

Rand hunched down as lead walked all over his cover. He saw the barkeep plainly now as he moved across in front of a sandstone boulder. The man fired as Rand lifted up swiftly, rifle rising, snapping two fast shots. The 'keep twisted violently, fell face first against the rock, bounced off and dropped, unmoving.

By now the man from the right had reached the campsite, leapt over the downed Milt, and kicked the tangled bedding into the V made by the rocks that sheltered Rand.

Rand wasn't expecting that and he fired even as the blankets and some of his clothes fouled the muzzle. The shot was muffled, and the cloth jerked and snagged the foresight. By then the killer was coming in after the bedroll, shooting. He tripped on the rope and his bullet screamed away, showering Rand with stinging grit. He wrenched the rifle barrel free of the clothes and spun towards his attacker. But the man was good, realized he was too close and in too cramped a position to risk triggering again. He reversed his hold on his carbine and slammed at Rand with the butt. The blow numbed his arm and he dropped his gun, kicked out even as he raised a hand to parry the next blow. His boot sank into the attacker's belly and the man gagged as he stumbled forward. Rand brought up a knee into his descending face and felt the nose squash, the jar as big teeth raked his knee cap. He clubbed downwards with a fist, delivering it like a hammer blow, and the killer's legs splayed untidily. He sprawled on his face and Rand kicked him once in the head, rolled away, groping for his rifle. He found it and reared to his knees.

The one called Milt was struggling to rise. Rand took a long step forward and clubbed him down. The barkeep was trying to bring up his six-gun. Rand fired swiftly and the 'keep dropped flat, fingers clawing desperately into the soil.

Breathing hard, Rand looked around at the sprawled bodies. In the glow of the scattered coals he saw all three were either dead, unconscious, or distressed enough to do little more than moan.

Rifle in his left hand, he kicked the firewood together, knelt on one knee and fanned the coals with his hat. He had a small blaze going in a minute. He grabbed each intruder by his shirt collar and dragged him into the circle of firelight. Milt was dead; the barkeep was wounded in a couple of places, and bleeding, but alive, though the fight had gone out of him. The third man, Jerry, sagged against a rock, his mutilated face catching the flickering light, reflecting from blood and mangled lips.

There was not much fight left in him either.

Rand propped his rifle against a rock, the muzzle resting in a small protrusion so it wouldn't fall and maybe discharge.

He rested his hips against a rock, rolled a cigarette, giving them a chance to get their wits about them. When the smoke was going, he addressed the barkeep, nudging him with a boot.

'Why'd you buy into this?'

The man lifted a pain-filled face but came up with a scowl and an obscene suggestion. Rand shook his head amiably.

'Not acrobatic enough to do that.'

His boot nudged the man harder and brought a quick moan from him. 'What's your name?'

The 'keep was gasping in pain, looked up this time with half-hooded eyes. His lips moved and Rand laughed briefly.

'Reckon your ma never called you that. Name don't matter. *Why* does. Last chance to tell me.'

He picked up a short, glowing stick from the edge of the fire, little flames licking at the end. The barkeep reared back as Rand made a pass at his face.

'Christ! Don't! Name's Lew. Milt an' Jerry were goin' after you, asked me to join 'em. Jer reckoned you were just stallin', tryin' to divert attention.'

'How's that?'

'Figured you — you found the loot Feeney stole, maybe stashed it some-place before bringin' . . . him in . . . an' claimin' the . . . bounty as . . . well.'

'*If* I'd found the loot, I just might've rode off with it and left Feeney in the canyon.'

Jerry spoke for the first time, his words slurred because of his busted mouth. 'An' pass up eleven hundred bucks . . . ?'

'Twelve thousand would've satisfied me, I reckon.'

'An' I . . . I reckon . . . you're a liar!'

Rand lifted his rifle and Jerry stiffened. 'Jerry, just shut up. Both of you listen. I'm gonna leave you here. No guns, no food, no horses.' They protested as best they could and he let them run down. 'That's how it's going to be. There's the waterhole, or, if you feel chipper enough, I crossed a stage trail just before noon. You might make it that far and grab a lift back to Columbine.'

'Judas Priest! That's . . . the stage only runs . . . once a week along that trail!'

'You'll be mighty hungry by then, I guess. Catch some lizards. I've et 'em before. Taste terrible but could keep you alive.'

'You can't . . . do it!' the barkeep

griped. 'I'm bleedin' to death!'

'Take the bandage off your hand and wad it over the bullet wounds. Look, gents, I got no sympathy for you. You aimed to kill me, whether I told you where I was s'posed to have stashed Feeney's loot or not. You make it back, OK. You don't . . . ? Have to tell you I won't lose any sleep wondering about it.'

'B-but — you can't just leave us!'

'Your horses'll likely find you. They'll come in for water. You'll have to try an' talk 'em into coming close enough for you to grab. Guess there's grub in your saddle-bags. Was aiming to take it when I find where you stashed your mounts, but I'll leave it and you just have to hope they wander up this way for a drink — that's as generous as I aim to be.'

He began gathering his bedroll and clothes.

'Where you . . . headed?' Rand merely looked at Jerry as the man asked. 'No, listen. I been here before, spent a deal of time in the Strip. Had to lay low for a spell once. I know trails, settlements. I can tell you where to find the caves some of the really wild boys live in. You leave us grub an' a gun. It don't have to be loaded, just toss some bullets down slope and we'll get to 'em later. But we gotta have some protection, man! Some of the fellers livin' in here'll find us! They'll use us for target practice — or toss us off the cliff an' bet on how long it'll take us to hit bottom! I *know* the kinda scum they are. We gotta do a deal!'

'You've got nothing to deal with, Jerry. I can find my way around without your help.' Rand studied the man: he was desperate. Obviously he and Lew were mighty afraid of being left to die. And Rand was counting on that fear to make them trade information for food and a gun.

Lew just lay there, looking from one man to the other, in obvious pain and an increasing state of anxiety. 'Tell him, Jer! Tell him what he wants to know!'

'Christ, I *dunno* what he wants to . . . know!' Jerry said, though he sensed Rand's desire for information of some kind. His eyes grew large as Rand remained silent.

After a time, when he had finished his cigarette, Rand said, 'Either of you know a man named Riley Duggan?'

'Judas!' breathed Lew, looking quickly at Jerry.

Jerry smiled crookedly. 'Hey, I reckon we got us a deal! Riley was the one helped hide me. I know where he hangs out. I can tell you — if you'll give us your word to leave us some grub and stuff.'

Rand let them sweat a little more, then nodded, keeping his face deadpan, hiding a growing feeling of excitement now. He stood, resting a hand on the butt of his six-gun, and said flatly,

'Start talking, Jerry. You've got yourself a deal.'

5

Outlaw country

Chet Rand reined in the roan swiftly, guided it into the shelter of some brush that overhung the barely discernible trail.

'Goddamn you, Jerry Whoever you are!' he said aloud in a low voice. 'You *lied* to me!'

Cautiously, he used his rifle barrel to ease aside some of the brush. Afternoon sunlight squinted up his eyes as he stared at the ring of rocks that clung to the mountain slope below him, overlooking the trail he should've taken — *would*'ve taken if he had followed Jerry's directions.

There were two men with rifles on guard down there.

He'd stopped to drink at a spring and a frilled dragon lizard had startled the roan. It had run off and he had chased it on foot — no choice! The only thing he was grateful for was that it didn't whinny after that first fright. But it weaved and zigzagged and must have run near half a mile before it slowed and turned to look at him, snorting and pawing the ground, shaking its head, waiting for him to approach.

He was ready for it to turn and run as it had on three previous occasions, but by now it had calmed down and allowed him to grab the reins.

'I oughta — wallop you good!' he gasped, then he saw the blood on the roan's left forefoot. 'Hell, boy! That damn lizard or whatever it was *bit* you! No wonder you took off.'

They were near some boulders and he led the animal in amongst them and washed the wound. It wasn't bad but there were six teeth marks oozing blood. He decided it would be best to allow it to bleed a little; not knowing what filth a scavenging lizard had been eating.

He sat down and smoked a cigarette. When he was ready to move, he realized he didn't know where the hell he was. He'd gotten turned around while chasing the roan and he couldn't pick out the landmarks Jerry had given him. He could hear the sounds of a river somewhere near, too, wild water, and Jerry hadn't even mentioned *that*.

He wasn't entirely a fool; he had been wary of Jerry's apparent willingness to give him detailed directions and he had travelled accordingly. Jerry wasn't the kind who would tell the truth if a lie would suffice, so, vindictively, he had sent Rand off on a series of trails that would put him right in the gunsights of those outlaw guards. But, luckily, his horse had run off to this high spot.

He was a little alarmed now, though he figured he could likely work out a direction again when it was dark and stars appeared. But he didn't want to hang around these parts. For all he knew he might be close to one of the main outlaw trails. So, on foot, he retraced some of the meandering tracks he and the roan had left, climbed a rock and, belly tightening, stood up, hoping there was no one above.

He saw a faint trail, going upslope, in the direction he wanted to travel, but he knew it wasn't the one Jerry had described; it looked disused, abandoned long ago.

Still, he decided to follow it, mighty warily, and see where it led.

Half an hour later he figured he was too high, well above the trail Jerry had described. Then he glimpsed a section of that trail through a heavy wall of brush, a couple of hundred feet below his present position.

Studying the lie of the land, he figured that if he went over the rise it would take him down to that trail below, where it swung around a spur, on the far side.

He was confident enough — until he came to the overhanging brush and paused to wipe sweat out of his eyes.

That was when he saw the two men below, in amongst a nest of rocks that made a virtual natural fort in miniature, overlooking the very trail Jerry had told him was quite safe, totally unguarded. It looked like a permanent guard post down there: a lean-to, rock fire-place, a trampled area where the men moved about the camp, a rough brush shelter for the mounts and gear.

Jerry must've known damn well there were armed men watching, just where any rider below would appear around a tight bend, a perfect target, at a point where the trail was too narrow to turn his mount, while they picked him off. And they would shoot without warning, aim to kill.

These men were protecting the approaches to their hideout and if they didn't recognize you as a friend, then you had to be an enemy.

And they would make you a dead enemy quicker than a flea could jump.

'I'll be seeing you again, Jerry, you lying sonuver!' Rand quietly promised himself as he looked for a safe way around those armed guards. 'It'll be better for you if you just die of thirst or your wounds, because when I catch up with you . . . '

There was little profit in thinking about that now.

He had been mighty lucky, thanks to that lizard.

Now he had to push what luck he had left in order to stay alive and get past those guards without being seen.

He took his field glasses from his saddle-bag, easing down amongst the rocks and focusing on the country beyond the guard post, hands cupped so they shaded the lenses. Long since, he had painted the brass cylinders black so they would not flash in the sun and warn mustangs he was hunting. It had paid off when he was searching for Feeney, too. Somewhere along the way, the left lens had cracked off-centre and this caused some distortion, but not enough to worry him.

He swept the glasses across the guard

post: it was manned by two beard-shagged men in grimy clothes, with lank, long, dirty hair — the look of men living wild. Their rifles were beside them as they played a hand of cards, using worn and greasy pasteboards. One man was discarding from his hand with sharp gestures that told Rand he was angry — likely losing.

'Enjoy yourselves, *amigos*,' he murmured. 'Argue with each other — give me time to take a decent look-see.'

There was a way down from where he was perched right now, but he would have to wait until dark. He could discern a route that would allow him to skirt the rear of the small butte where the men were stationed. Looking at the set-up, he figured the same men likely did a two- or three-day stint at a time on guard, maybe longer. So they would be sleeping here tonight — well, at least one would be sleeping while the other stood guard, if they were really serious. Or, maybe not.

Playing cards as they were now didn't

exactly mark them down as keen, duty-bound watchmen.

With men like these he couldn't take the risk; he would have to watch each step as if both men were awake and sharp-witted, alert to every small sound in the night.

It was a steep slope, and the horse was bound to slip and slide at some time, even though Rand himself would be afoot and leading by the reins, using his weight and balance to control both himself and the roan on their descent.

But there was no choice. Unless he picked both guards off from here right now while they were totally unaware of him.

Stupid! Gunfire would echo through this country like a train roaring through a cutting, the sound bouncing from ridge to ridge, rock to rock, deadfall to . . .

No, it would have to be the hard way. So he tore up his blanket and wrapped the now placid roan's hoofs in as many layers as he could, tying the cloth in place with some of the short lengths of rope he had originally prepared for taking in Feeney as a prisoner. He had just enough left over to wrap around his own boots to help deaden the sound as he stumbled downslope in the dark.

His thumping heart would still be jammed in the back of his throat, no matter what — it was already racing faster than normal.

He pulled the roan into some deeper shade and settled down to wait for night to sweep over these mountains. He couldn't risk a cigarette, certainly not a campfire. But his belly was growling; he rummaged in his bags and found a few strips of leathery jerky. That and a mouthful of canteen water would be his meal tonight.

If breakfast was the same he wouldn't complain, as long he was around to *have* breakfast.

* * *

He almost made it.

The night was black as a preacher's cassock but the stars blazed magnificently and gave enough light for him to see obstacles a few yards ahead — in some cases only a few feet. And one time, too late: the ground dropped away from beneath him, and he was falling with half a ton of loose soil trying to bury him.

Worse, the roan fell, too, toppling on its side, hoofs kicking instinctively. In panic, the animal was whinnying shrilly, the sound piercing the night. Rand slid and skidded, choking in the dust. As he reached the bottom he rolled over and over, as swiftly as possible, aware several hundred pounds of thrashing horse was only seconds behind and above him.

He caught one hoof in the back, felt it rip his shirt and the breath *whumped* out of him briefly. He covered his head with his arms instinctively for protection.

But the roan was staggering and

grunting to its feet, standing there, snorting, sneezing dust and grit out of distended nostrils. Rand stood carefully, brushing himself down, stooped to pick up his crushed hat and punched it into shape. He coughed and spat, breath coming hard as he looked around in the dim light. He gave a crooked grin and stepped forward, rubbing the quivering mount's forehead and scratching behind one ear.

'We took the tumble together that time, boy.' He quickly checked the horse's legs and body for injuries, found a couple of strips of grazed hide — he had a couple himself, too — but otherwise the roan had escaped serious hurt.

They were now at the foot of the steep slope, a big blob of shapeless brush masking what he hoped would be the continuation of the trail. He decided to mount and ride the rest of the way; it seemed clear enough and he would keep the horse at walking pace, anyway.

Just as he lifted one boot into the stirrup, standing one-legged, a cold voice said, 'Now you just hold it like that, feller! Just keep doing that balancin' act and your head might stay on your shoulders a couple minutes longer. Savvy?'

Rand stayed put but could feel the roan all tensed, waiting for him to complete the mounting process. Puzzled when nothing happened, the horse moved — and Rand had to hop to stay upright. Inevitably, the horse moved faster than he could dance on one leg. His boot pulled free of the oxbow and he tumbled to the ground.

He had enough time to roll on to his back, then a heavy boot pinned him painfully by the shoulder and he found himself looking into the dark maw of a rifle barrel.

'Man, you are one lucky son of a bitch!' the outlaw growled. 'I'd've blowed you in two except we want to know how the *hell* you got past our guards! An' if you went around 'em, then we damn well want to know how you done that, too!'

'Do I get to keep my head then?' Rand asked, breathless, hands level with his shoulders now.

A boot thudded into his ribs and the man standing above him called softly, 'You comin' in, Rile? I got the bastard.'

'On my way,' a voice answered out of the darkness and a minute later a big man, as tall as Rand but wider in the shoulders and thicker round the middle appeared beside the rifleman. A six-gun gleamed in his fist as he stooped down to get a better look at Rand. His other hand came around and the thumbnail snapped a match into flame. Rand reared back, squinting in the flaring light, arm lifting across his eyes.

The big man had shut his eyes momentarily to miss that blinding flash. Now he knocked the arm aside and peered closely at his prisoner.

'Know him?' asked the rifleman.

'No-oo. But think I saw him headin' towards Columbine a day or so back.

Had a dead man roped over his pack hoss but I wasn't close enough to see who it was. Reckon it could've been Feeney.'

'This the sonuver that killed Feen, then?' The rifle lifted an inch and the big man shook out the match and pushed the weapon away from Rand.

'I think so. How about it, feller? You that bounty hunter?'

'I'm not a pro, but I was hunting Feeney. I need a thousand bucks and — '

The rifleman kicked him in the ribs, making him draw his knees up to his chest. 'Damn you! I liked Feeney!'

Rand pressed a hand into his throbbing side. 'I'm beginning to think he was mighty popular round these parts, even if he did have a dodger out on him.'

'Hell, Feen weren't no real outlaw,' the big man said. 'He liked poker, was his main problem. Poker and women.'

'Sounds normal enough.'

The big man chuckled. 'Good to hear

83

you agree. He lifted a few bucks when he needed it but he never hurt no one. More'n one time he just gave up an' left without a red cent when he figured the other feller was gonna get hardnosed about it an' maybe go for a gun.'

Rand shook his head slowly. 'Well, he doesn't sound like a real hardcase. I'm glad I never killed him.'

That earned him another boot in the side. 'You start lyin' mister, and you'll be talkin' through a mouthful of busted teeth!'

'Christ! Ease up on my ribs, will you? Look, I thought I was shooting it out with him but he was already dead — '

'*He was what?*'

He flinched as the rifleman drew back a boot but the big man stalled him and he didn't deliver the kick.

'The hell're you talkin' about? 'Already dead?' '

Rand told it as it had happened and could just make out the look his captors exchanged.

'Who the hell you reckon that other feller could be, Rile?'

'Well, Feen's been hintin' he wanted a pard for somethin' he had in mind. Could be he picked a wrong 'un.'

'That's if you believe him!' The rifleman managed to get in his kick this time and Riley pushed him away.

'Ease up, Blake! I want to know how he come to be here, an' how he got past Hendy and Marsh.'

'They'll be lookin' for us, too, Rile. We're kinda late relievin' 'em.'

'They can wait. This is important. You — what's your name?' Rand told him. 'All right, Rand, you know what we want to know. How the hell did you get past that roadblock? And how come you got so far into the Strip?'

'You know a pair in Columbine — barkeep named Lew, and a hardcase calls himself Jerry?'

'Them two!' grated Blake. 'Told you we oughta stop dealin' with 'em! They shoot their mouth off too damn easy!'

'How come they talked to you? You

use a hot runnin'-iron on 'em, or somethin'?'

'No. But I'd wounded 'em both. Killed their sidekick, Milt.' The man stepped back a little, wary now. Rand nodded to Blake. 'Heard him call you 'Rile'. You Riley Duggan?'

'Where'd you hear that name?' the big man asked quietly, a certain tension edging the words.

Rand hesitated, then saw that the man, who hadn't yet admitted being Riley Duggan in so many words, had cocked his pistol now. It was aimed at his left kneecap.

'Don't like to get a lady into trouble, but — ' he began, but he was interrupted.

'Lady? If you mean who I think you mean, then you're a mite off-target, man. She's no 'lady', but the only one likely to get you started in my direction. We talkin' about Ginger Holt?'

Rand nodded. 'She was in the bushes while you were holding Feeney's getaway mounts and heard him call you 'Riley'.'

Blake was staring at his pard, mouth sagging. 'You never said — '

''Cause I never held no getaway mounts!' cut in Duggan. 'Can you see me holdin' the getaway mounts for anyone? Man, I got a hundred of you ham-'n'-eggers to hold my getaway broncs, or polish my shoes, fetch my booze . . . ' He drew back a boot and Rand squirmed again in an attempt to get out of range. But the big man lowered his foot slowly. Then he surprised him by grinning, turning towards Blake.

'That bitch! We had a fallin'-out, and I belted her one that knocked her halfway across her damn room!' He moved restlessly as if he would like to throw himself into the night and smash something. 'Goddamn her! See what she's done? Named me as Feeney's sidekick! Gettin' her own back!' He made a growling noise through clenched teeth. 'Hell, this gets back to Powers and that sonuver'll have a posse over here lookin' for me, legal or not!'

'Could be right, Rile,' Blake allowed and poked Rand with his rifle barrel. 'But what about him? He's found his way in here — and right into our own territory!'

Riley Duggan drew in a deep breath, nodding. 'You born lucky? Or Jerry tell you a way how to dodge my guards?'

'Lucky?' Rand asked from the ground. 'Lying here with you two standing over me with loaded guns, kicking my ribs up around my ears — that makes me lucky?'

'You're still breathin', ain't you?'

'I — think I see what you mean. Yeah, guess you could say I'm lucky at that.' He told them how the horse had run off just before he would have reached the guard post and how, seeing the men, he had cut up over the crest.

'That old Injun trail,' Blake allowed. 'We'll have to blast it, Rile. We been gonna do it for long enough.'

Riley Duggan nodded. 'You're right. We'll do it tomorrow. Just in case

Powers does come sniffin' around. Now, Rand, why the hell you come lookin' for me?'

'Told you, Powers still thinks I backshot Feeney despite Doc Swanson proving different. I figured if you had been Feeney's pard in that stage robbery, and I could take you back — '

Blake guffawed. 'Hell almighty! You take Riley Duggan back to that snotty sheriff in Columbine? What the hell you been drinkin', boy?'

Rand smiled crookedly. 'Seems I might've been a bit over-confident, you reckon?'

'Could say that.' Riley Duggan spoke thoughtfully. 'S'pose I had been Feeney's sidekick and I had that twelve thousand dollars, what'd you aim to do? Take it and me in and claim the bounty? Or kill me and keep the twelve thousand dollars — ten times the reward?'

Rand hesitated. Then, 'I hadn't planned to kill you, but — well, guess I might've been tempted to offer to split the twelve grand with you.'

Blake and Riley looked at each other and Duggan smiled, offering Rand a hand to help him to his feet:

'Always like an honest man — even if he's thinkin' of bein' dishonest. Reckon you an' me better have a talk, Rand.'

6

The Pit

Chet Rand was surprised to see as many as twenty outlaws in Riley's hideout, an abandoned lumber camp. The cleared slopes were still dotted with many weathered old tree stumps and even a crumbling sawpit, half-full of mouldy sawdust. The men were gathered round several campfires.

They looked like what they were: lawless men living rough. Suspicious, dark, probing eyes watched Rand's every movement. A couple admired the dust-spattered roan. The horses he saw in a big set of corrals were varied, some in good condition, others hard-used, and never going to improve, still others that should be resting-up or put out to pasture permanently. But here, in outlaw country, they had to work mighty hard for every mouthful of hay; there was grass, but it had obvioulsy been heavily grazed over the years and appeared mostly in brownish tufts.

There were lean-tos, a couple of tents, several crude log huts, and two more made of sod with grass growing thickly on the roof. He glimpsed some feminine underwear flapping on a washline and saw pale skin and knotty hair at a sod hut window, a brush trying to untangle the dull strands.

'All the comforts of home,' Riley said, dragging Rand, whose hands were tied, off the roan. 'But none for you. Least not yet — an' only if you're a good boy, OK?'

Rand shifted his boots to steady himself on the ground, his shoulder brushing his horse. He held up his bound wrists. 'This ain't necessary.'

''Tis if I say so.' Duggan turned as several of the outlaws wandered across to get a look at Rand; because his hands were bound they figured he was suspect right now: a lawman trying to sneak in?

A stranger who had stumbled on one of the hidden trails and been dragged in because . . . ?

That was what intrigued them: most strangers were usually shot on sight — so why was this one still alive?

'*Amigos*, meet Chet Rand, bounty-hunter. Killed Feeney, but Brock Powers won't pay the bounty, 'cause Feen was backshot.'

That brought some murmurs and at least two of the watchers dropped hands to gun butts. Not that *they* would have any compunction about shooting a man in the back, but to have it happen to one of their own — well, almost one of their own, seeing as Feeney was a half-hearted outlaw — by a goddamn bounty hunter, the profession most hated by these men . . .

That riled.

A lanky, bony red-haired man with a fringe of sparse sandy beard walked up to Rand and looked at him with hard eyes. He kept staring and Rand didn't avert his gaze. Then suddenly the redhead's fist drove into Rand's midriff. He gusted breath, stumbled and dropped to one knee. Another man stepped in and raised his gun to club him but Riley snapped, 'Hold it! We gotta question him some.'

The second outlaw, heavily built, but squat, giving a toadlike impression, grinned. 'Now that sounds more like it. I got dibs on the first five minutes!' He flicked his gaze around at the men now crowding in. 'There might not be any need for a *second* five minutes, of course!'

'There will be,' Riley Duggan cut in, hauling Rand to his feet, the man still bent in the middle, fighting for breath. 'I need to know somethin' and he's gotta be able to talk, so Blake an' me'll do the questionin'.' There were growls and hard looks but he held up a hand casually. 'When we get what we want, you can have him for target practice.'

Rand snapped his head up, startled, the grimace of pain disappearing. 'Wha— ? What the hell, Duggan?'

'You'll find out. Dump him outside my hut while I wash up. And guard him. Someone off-saddle his hoss, too. He won't be needin' it again.'

Rand felt dazed even before they dragged him up the slope and dumped him against the peeled-log wall of one of the cabins. The redhead and the toadlike man stood over him. Red spat on him.

'My old man was backshot by a lousy bounty hunter. You're the first I've met since then, Rand.'

'Lucky — me,' Rand gasped and doubled up as he took two hard kicks in the back, under the shoulders. The world spun in and out of focus and he felt as if he was dying, unable to take in enough breath. But it gradually settled and the roaring in his ears diminshed, the red haze lifted slowly from behind his eyes.

So he was able to see Riley Duggan standing in front of him, wiping his face with a ragged towel.

'What the hell you want from me? I

can't tell you anything.'

Riley squatted in front of him, rubbing his dripping hair, long and curly. 'You only think you can't. You gonna be s'prised just what you'll tell me before I'm through.'

Rand didn't like the sound of that.

★ ★ ★

The trouble was, Riley Duggan had a mighty devious mind, and he tended to figure that anyone walking the edge of the law must think the same way he did. Which, he allowed, was the only way to stay clear of the lawmen and the double-crossers amongst other inhabitants of the Cherokee Strip.

This is how he explained it to Rand:

'I reckon you might've found that loot and stashed it someplace, Rand.'

'*When*, for Chris'sakes? I only caught up with Feeney in that dead-end canyon and it turned out he was already dead — was his pard who did the back-shooting.'

'Well, that's as mebbe.' Duggan lifted a hand. 'Not sayin' it couldn't be just the way you told it. What I *am* sayin' is that I can't afford to take a chance on it. I gotta make sure, damn sure, you ain't usin' all this eyewash just to throw Powers — and me — off your track.'

Rand writhed in his bonds. 'Hell almighty, I've come up against some devious sonuvers over the years, dealing with mustangers and shysters trying to bluff me into admitting I took my catch off their land. But I don't think I've ever come across anyone with your imagination! And that includes a feller interviewed me once for the *Denver Post* — and I tell you, he had a mighty wild imagination: I didn't even recognize myself in the story he wrote.'

He grunted and rolled as Blake hit him across the side of the head with a length of firewood. He was away with the birdies and the showering meteors for a few minutes and when he came back, head thudding, he tasted blood, too. His eyes seemed to roll loosely, like kid's marbles in a cup.

'You don't speak, 'less you're sayin' what we want to hear!' Blake snapped, slapping him backhanded once more.

Riley Duggan, straddling a log just outside the cabin door, signed to Blake to ease off. 'Let him think about it a spell. He'll see we're bein' reasonable.'

'I'd hate to — see you on an *unreasonable* day,' Rand gasped and Riley laughed.

'Like your sense of humour, Rand!' He hitched a little closer. 'Look, we're talkin' twelve thousand bucks here, not some piss-ant kid's pocket money. If Feeney had a pard, it'd be unusual. An' don't take no notice of Ginger. She'll come round eventually and be all over me like a poison-ivy rash. She's hair-trigger, see? Fires off an' says anythin' comes into her head. So, just forget her. I was nowhere near that stage robbery and sure not Feen's pard.'

'Someone was. He shot Feeney in the back.'

'So you say. And even if that sawbones was right about the bullet calibres, still don't mean you didn't have two different rifles.'

Rand made an exasperated jerk of his head. 'I didn't! I've used that rifle in my saddle scabbard for months, .45 calibre. It's the only one I've got. You keep on like this, Riley, and we'll get nowhere.'

Duggan had a leafy switch in his hand, waving it around to keep off the mosquitoes. He whipped it across Rand's face, leaving several short welts and one long one. There was no animosity or anger in his voice when he spoke again.

'See, I've knowed Feeney for a long time. A piker when it came to hold-ups. He'd run if someone reached under a counter, or fumbled for tobacco in his pocket. The original Nervous Nellie. Twelve thousand would've knocked him cock-eyed after all the small change he'd been used to. He wouldn't know what to do — so he'd run, run someplace where he could be by himself, afraid of his own shadow, expectin' someone was gonna jump out and take that *dinero* from him.'

Duggan leaned close and Rand eased back, expecting the switch again. But the outlaw simply shook his head.

'He wouldn't let go of that twelve grand! He'd have it with him, would be too scared to stash it in case someone found it. See what I'm gettin' at? You nailed him while he was on the run, so he *must've had the loot with him*!'

Rand spoke slowly, gritting his teeth 'If he did — then whoever shot him in the back took it off him before I got there! He had no more'n a handful of change when I found him.'

'Yeah, well that's possible, too — but only *if* someone else backshot him.'

'Ah, for Chris'sake!' Rand shook his head, although his brain seemed loose in his skull. 'I'm gonna die under torture and I still won't be able to tell you *any goddamn different*! Can't you get that through your thick skull?'

Riley's eyes narrowed and he held

Blake back as the man started to move in. He stood slowly, hitched his pants and then looked down at Rand. 'You only think you won't.' He raised his voice. 'You ladies in there, get to cookin' supper. I'm hungry.' He glanced down at Rand once more and smiled crookedly. 'An' I'm about to work up a big appetite, so you cook up plenty, hear?'

Blake jerked Rand to his feet, looking expectantly at Duggan. 'Sawpit?'

'Why the hell not? We can bury him under all that sawdust if he dies before we get finished.'

Boots dragging, Rand was cuffed and kicked and spat on by several of the outlaws as they made their way towards the dark maw of the saw pit. He saw, by the light of one fire, a grey-haired man sitting on a log outside one of the sod huts, crimping detonators into sticks of dynamite, using his teeth to do it.

'Hey, Slat. You cain't be that hungry!' someone called. 'The gals are cookin' supper now. Even the slop they serve's gotta taste better'n a stick of dynamite! Safer, too. It'll leave your head on your shoulders!'

The grey-haired man grinned and spat. ''Less it poisons you. I'll take me chances.'

He carelessly tossed a prepared stick into an open box where several others were lying, fuses sticking up like wire.

'You make them fuses longer, Slats!' Blake said as they passed. 'I wanta come back with both hands after blastin' that trail.'

'Try livin' dangerously, Blake! The only way — an' look at me.' He lifted both hands. 'Been doin' it for years an' still got all my fingers.'

'But not all your brains. *You* can blast the trail. I ain't gonna risk it with short fuses.'

Slats laughed derisively.

Blake shoved Rand's shoulder, making him stagger, and called back, 'Just don't start blastin' too early. Reckon I'll be mighty tired after the exercise I'm gonna get tonight! An' I don't mean with one of them whores!'

He laughed harshly and deliberately tripped Rand.

★ ★ ★

Rand had once read about the pyramids of Egypt and the millions of tons of rock that had been used to build them.

He felt like he was lying under the biggest pyramid when his puffy eyes flickered open.

He coughed and spat, tasting old blood, feeling cuts inside his mouth, his teeth aching and some loose in the gums. His nose was clogged with congealed blood. His body . . . we-ee-lll . . .

Once, a long time ago, when he was learning the hard way how to break in mustangs he had trapped, he had been bucked off this big, rolling-eyed claybank, and it had tried to stomp him. It was a mean son of a bitch and lay down and tried to roll on him. He was only partly successful in escaping and spent weeks with his ribs and one arm in plaster.

Right now, he felt as if the damn stallion and his whole blamed harem had rolled over him. Riley Duggan and Blake sure liked to use their boots, seemed to back up every blow from their fists with a barrage of kicks. They dragged him and slammed him violently against the hard-earth walls of the sawpit, one holding him while the other set his boots firmly and slogged away until he was breathless.

Rand was unconscious by then, of course, but they sloshed a bucket of water over him — slop-water from the whores' laundry or dishwashing — then started all over. They let him lie and just when he thought he was getting a breathing space, they started kicking him all round the pit, across and under and through the accumulated depth of stinking sawdust. Half-blinded, half-choked, he heard Riley's voice as if coming down a

deep well — with him at the bottom:
'Where's that twelve thousand?'

Rand didn't have enough breath even to deny he knew.

'Jesus, my hands're gettin' sore!' Duggan complained, rubbing his stiff fingers and sucking split knuckles.

'Got me an idea,' Blake panted, moving to climb out of the pit. 'Drag him across on that high pile of sawdust and stand him up. He's tall enough to see over the edge.'

'The hell're you doin'?'

Blake was standing on the edge of the pit now. 'Come on, Riley. Get him up here. He'll be talkin' in about three minutes.'

He moved out of sight and Duggan cursed, grunted and strained to lift the groggy, half-conscious Rand so his head was just above the pit level. Riley strained to see what Blake was up to as well. He tensed.

Blake was bringing Rand's roan from the corrals, had a rope hackamore over its head. 'Can he see?'

'Well, his head's above ground level.'

'Good. Rand? Lookee here!'

His six-gun came up and Riley yelled, '*No!* You blamed fool! That'll only . . . '

Too late. The gunshot was muffled as the muzzle was rammed into the roan's left ear. The big horse seemed to jump, its forelegs crossing, head twisting violently. Blake leapt aside as it crashed over, kicking and shuddering.

'Ah, goddamnit!' Riley Duggan gritted, feeling Rand's battered body go as rigid as an iron bar.

He heard the guttural sounds deep in Rand's chest as he struggled to find words enough to spit at the smug Blake. And when he did manage to speak, his voice was harsh, gasping, frightening.

'I'll — kill you the — same — way, Blake — count on — it!'

His legs were giving way and Riley flung him back to slide down the slope of sawdust, half-buried at the foot of the pile. Duggan clambered out as

Blake holstered his pistol, standing beside the dead horse. He walked across — and smashed his fist into the middle of Blake's startled face.

The man staggered back, tripped over one of the roan's legs and sprawled in the dust. Men had come running and stood silent now, watching as Duggan towered above the dazed Blake, who blinked up through a screen of blood.

'The — hell . . . ?'

Duggan kicked him hard, dropped a hand to his gun butt as Blake grunted and started to reach for his own Colt.

'Go on! Drag it, and I'll finish you!'

Blake let his hand fall away from the butt, struggled to sit up, mopping his face with a grimy kerchief, holding it to his gushing nostrils. 'Why, for Chris'sakes?'

Riley couldn't stand still, he was so angry. He paced around Blake who watched apprehensively, knowing how ruthless and vicious Duggan could be when he was riled up.

'You blamed *idiot*! You just clamped

Rand up like a blacksmith had stapled his lips together! Judas priest! We could've used the damn horse to *make* him talk.'

'I thought I — just did.'

'Shut up, Blake!' Duggan placed his gun barrel against Blake's head and the man froze. Those watching held their breaths. But Duggan didn't drop the hammer. 'We could have *threatened* to kill the roan unless he told us what we want to know. Dunno why I never thought of it from the start. Anyone could see he was partial to that jughead. Now it's too late! The horse is dead and we won't get a goddamn word outta him!'

Blake frowned, blinked. 'I-I din' think of it like that, Rile. Just figured killin' the roan would shake him up an' . . . '

Duggan rammed his gun into his holster and turned towards his hut with angry strides. 'Make sure the son of a bitch is tied up proper and leave him 'til mornin'. We been too soft with him.

Time to get out the brandin'-iron.'

Lying half-buried in stinking damp sawdust, Rand heard this — and knew there was not a blamed thing he could do about it.

★ ★ ★

He played possum when a couple of rannies dropped into the pit and dragged him out from under the sawdust, flinging him into a corner by the saw jig. The long rusted blade gleamed dully as one said, 'His hands are still tied — s'pose we better rope his feet, eh?'

'Yeah — that'll do. An' hurry it up. I can smell that stew them whores are cookin' and it's loaded with chilli, just the way I like it.'

★ ★ ★

Rand had passed out fully. When he came round, he felt a crushing weight on him and he looked up past the angles and framework of the big saw jig, stars burning high up over the edge of the pit.

There was no sound from the outlaws' camp although he had vague recollections of earlier hearing drunken singing and raucous voices raised in anger, men cheering on a fight. Or maybe he had dreamt it, though he recollected seeing what he thought was a liquor still down near the sod huts as they had dragged him towards the sawpit earlier.

He groaned involuntarily. Ropes were biting into his swollen hands, more bonds clamped his ankles together. He was surprised no one had taken his boots yet — must be waiting until he was dead.

Like hell! That thought brought him out of his groggy, half-conscious state. Pain surged through him like a wave of acid from feet to scalp. He spat some thick, cloying matter that made him gag, tried to wipe his mouth on the sawdusted shoulder of his torn shirt. It hurt his neck and his head spun dizzily, ears ringing.

Time passed as he lay there, willing himself to push the pain away so he could *think*. He had to get out of here or he was a dead man — and it would be a mighty painful death, to no good purpose. He squirmed and wriggled, every fibre of his body screaming in its own brand of burning agony. He managed to roll away from the burying sawdust, lay gasping, with his face pushed into the trampled earth around the base of the saw jig. Once his boots hit the long blade, now sagging in its frame, and the metal rang dully.

It was several minutes later before that fact penetrated his throbbing brain.

The pit-saw! Rusted from disuse and lack of care, big, ripping teeth, bent and twisted — but still *sharp*.

He started to hitch around, using his bent legs painfully to drag his backside along the ground, inching closer to the base of the blade. His boots hit it and it rang like a church bell — or so it seemed to him. But the sound was confined to the pit and although it hurt his ears, he realized it would be barely heard above ground.

Still, he lay there, unmoving, gasping, chest heaving and hurting with every breath.

Then, when no one came running to investigate, he wrenched around painfully and worked his way up the short slope, the damp sawdust compressing with his weight, giving him something reasonably firm to rest on.

It was a struggle to turn around so his wrist ropes were against the battered teeth of the huge blade, and his shoulders and arms screamed as he started the first tentative movements, rubbing the ropes up and down. He smothered a cry of pain as rusted metal tore his flesh, moved a little, and then heard the harsh rasping as the fibres were severed, snapping one by one.

7

Exit Hell

The unmistakable smell of sourmash permeated the outlaw camp.

There were bodies sprawled all over the slope, lying where they had fallen in drunken stupor, limbs and brains paralysed by the rotgut spewed out by the big still between the sod huts. The fire beneath the cauldron was no more than glowing coals now; a little steam bubbled, each bursting membrane of thick liquid puffing up and increasing the smell of the mash. Someone had taken the condenser lid off and he saw a jug with congealing mash on its sides and handle.

They must have run out of distilled liquor and the damn fools were so far out of their brains they had scooped up the fermenting mash and half-drunk, half-chewed the mess.

It suited Rand: they would be sick and only interested in dying for a time when they eventually awoke.

He was unsteady on his feet, his clothes and hair were dusted with clinging sawdust, itching him under his shirt. His arms and hands still throbbed, the circulation not yet fully restored, streaked with blood from sawtooth cuts. As he stood swaying, looking at the results of the drunken orgy, he managed a crooked smile, although it hurt swollen and cut lips and his throbbing jaw. He peeked in the doors of the sod huts; the whores were as unconscious and uncaring as the men — two were spreadeagled on the floor, half-naked men's arms flung across their hard-used bodies.

Rand stumbled on, using the walls of the cabins to steady himself as he made his way past the roan's carcass to the brush-roofed horse shelter. The mounts were all in the corrals but there were saddle rigs lying around the shelter.

Groping, stopping once to vomit, he pawed over the untidy pile and found his own saddle. The rifle scabbard was still attached but the gun was gone. Disappointed, he turned away, caught his foot in something and sprawled, knocking down a hay fork with a clatter.

He lay prone, holding his breath. He thought the noise hadn't disturbed anyone, but as he started to get stiffly to his feet, a cracked, slurred voice called,

'You find any likker, I want some . . .'

He froze, ran a tongue over his battered lips, saw a man with disarrayed grey hair, pale in the light of the setting half-moon, stumble out of a cabin in his long underwear. Rand recognized him as Slats, the dynamite man.

'Who's it anyways?' Slats slurred as he swayed towards the brush shelter, straining to see. 'You, Puma . . . ?'

Rand, not moving now, grunted and Slats, still coming, chuckled. 'Yeah. Have to be you, you damn guzzler! Well, if you stashed somethin' away, I wants my share — someone's buried a blunt axe between my eyes.'

'He'p yourself,' slurred Rand, picking up a bottle, lying on its side. Slats saw the gleam of glass and rushed in, hands reaching. But Rand stepped aside and clipped the grey-haired man across the back of his neck, the bottle jarring. Slat dropped, out cold.

Rand doubled over, trying to get his breath, alarmed that even this small exertion had left him dizzy. He was never going to manage to get away in this condition! But he sure couldn't hide anywhere and give himself time to recover. He wouldn't dare try to catch a horse the way he was: stumbling, staggering, he'd only scare them and they'd start milling and whinnying and stomping.

'Well, I ain't stayin' here no matter what!'

He surprised himself, murmuring that aloud, waited tensely. No one came to the doors of the huts or yelled. None of the sprawled outlaws stirred, except one man near Slats' hut. And he only coughed, but . . .

Slats' hut! And primed dynamite ready to seal the old trail he had used to get around the guard post . . .

Hefting the bottle he had used on Slats, he heard liquid splashing around in the bottom. It was no doubt rotgut but he needed some kind of a boost. He put the bottle to his mouth and drank. It stung like hot lye and he gagged, but managed to swallow a mouthful. He fought for breath in rapid gasps, tracing the rotgut's descent into his stomach by a searing path down his gullet. He sat down heavily, tears running from his eyes. There was just a small amount left in the bottle and, taking a deep breath, he poured it down his throat. He struggled to keep from coughing and sat there, breathing through his mouth, the caress of night air welcome on his cut cheeks and tongue.

After several minutes, head buzzing now, belly on fire, he staggered upright. Gripping the bottle by its neck he warily edged into the hut. It stank and was black as the inside of a tar barrel. He groped with his left hand as he shuffled forward, barked his shin against something. Carefully, he reached down and snatched his hand back swiftly, thinking he had touched a snake.

It wasn't any kind of reptile: it was a short length of fuse. He had found the box of dynamite sticks Slats had prepared for the trail-sealing this morning.

Hand shaking now, he groped amongst the primed sticks remembering Slats had carelessly dropped a box of matches in amongst them after lighting a cheroot.

He found it, hesitated, then figured he had to have some light. He closed the cabin door, snapped his thumbnail against a vesta head and squinted quickly as it flared. He found a rickety table and an oil lamp, lit it and turned the wick low, leaving just enough light to see into the corners of the small, single room.

A battered old Colt hung in a worn leather holster and belt on a bent nail.

Only some of the loops carried cartridges but it would do. He strapped it on quickly, fumbling with his still tingling fingers. He couldn't see a rifle but figured he had better not push his luck and hang around. Old Slats might come to at any time.

The gun dragging at his waist, he picked up the box of dynamite, then saw a half-smoked cheroot, cold and mangled, resting on an old coffee-can lid that had obviously been used as an ash tray.

He jammed the butt between his aching teeth and fired it up. His head was already spinning from the moon-shine and the first drag of strong tobacco smoke made the room spin. He held the edge of the table just long enough to steady himself, then gathered up the box again and stumbled out through the door.

Slats was sitting up groggily and saw him. He just stared — and then, as Rand started towards Riley Duggan's cabin, he suddenly yelled in his cracked voice.

'Wake up! Wake up you blamed fools! We bein' robbed!'

Rand cursed him and grabbed a primed stick of dynamite, paused to steady himself a little so he could hold the end of the fuse to the glowing cheroot. Once it started to sputter he tossed it in Slats' general direction, seeing it fall well short, but Slats was prone on the ground by then. The second stick he tossed through the door of the hut he believed to be Duggan's, then he stumbled and staggered down the slope.

The first stick exploded, gouting earth and splintered poles and brush from the horse shelter. The second stick went off moments later, a different sound, yet still thunderous, though contained within the walls of the log cabin. The door blew off and shingles flew from the roof. The window shutters bulged and flung splintered wood into the night with a *whump-whumping* sound.

Rand fell, the box skidding out of his grasp. He rolled after it, reaching in for more sticks, but some had spilled out.

He was surprised at how quickly the 'dead' raised themselves out of their rotgut-induced stupor: likely long-used to coming awake pronto in any kind of emergency, living the way they did — and more tolerant of the moonshine than he had allowed.

Someone started shooting, though he didn't hear any of the bullets striking anywhere near him. He tossed another sputtering stick in the general direction of a cabin, glimpsed a trouserless man holding a shotgun in the doorway a second before the dynamite exploded and the man disappeared, along with the front of the cabin.

Bullets sought him then. He huddled low, dirt and grit erupting around him, some stinging his hands and neck. He stretched out, got one more fuse lit from the cheroot and tossed it aimlessly. He heard it explode somewhere behind him, felt the rush of torn air and heard the whizzing of rubble pattering down nearby.

'It's Rand!'

He felt his belly give a lurch: *Riley Duggan's voice!* The man had survived the dynamite blast: probably he hadn't even been in his cabin. He was swaying in the doorway of the whores' sod hut now, dishevelled and angry.

Rand threw the next stick towards the corrals. He knew it would have to be his last although there were still several in the box. Maybe the blast didn't knock down the brush fence, but it was close enough for the mounts to panic and try to leap over, smashing it flat.

The horses streamed out, whinnying, racing this way and that, scattering the drink-sodden outlaws. They got out of the way pronto, one man falling and starting to scream as the first line of hoofs thudded into his back. His yells were cut short and a bundle of torn, bloody rags was left as a dark smudge on the slope.

Rand was up and running — more like stumbling. But there was nothing like mortal fear to put power and speed into a man's limbs, even if he was half-dead from a sadistic beating.

Rand gave up counting the number of times he fell and rolled, but he was going downhill all the time and all hell was above him as the frantic horses raced through the camp and the men, most in their bare feet, strove desperately to get out of the way. Guns were rattling but he neither heard nor felt any of the bullets.

Righting himself after yet another fall, Rand put out a hand to rest against a boulder, dragging down deep breaths — or as deep as he could manage without his ribs and lungs feeling like a giant fist was clamping them.

Then he jumped and dropped instinctively to his knees as a bullet streaked silver across the rock just above his head, whined away in ricochet. The six-gun was in his hand and he searched for the shooter, found the man not ten yards away, only slightly above him.

His shirt hung in rags and it was obvious he had taken a tumble and rolled all the way down the slope from the cabin area. Rand didn't know who he was and didn't care. He snapped a shot at him and dropped prone as the outlaw fired again. Rand rolled over swiftly, across the slope, rather than down, which was the way the outlaw had naturally figured he would go. He had risen up and fired too quickly, the bullet striking two feet below his target.

Rand fired only once, conserving his ammunition. It was enough. The outlaw staggered and went down. Rand jumped down the slope then and dropped over a low ledge, even as several bullets chewed at the rocks.

He had been spotted and these men were in the mood for instant vengeance. Rolling, and skidding, he grabbed at stunted brush with his free hand, dug in his boots to slow his descent; the slope was much steeper than he had allowed.

A man appeared on the ledge, rifle in hand. He lifted it to his shoulder, levered and triggered, placing several close shots around Rand's still sliding body. As Rand came to rest, Blake's voice reached him through the pounding thunder in his head.

'Mebbe you'll find your roan in hell, Rand!'

The rifle whiplashed and the bullet seared Rand's back. As he heard Blake's lever clash again, he threw himself forward. It was a desperate move, for the slope dropped so steeply he didn't land on it until he had dropped several feet vertically.

He hit hard and flailed wildly, unable to stop now. His body bounced and skidded as the angle steepened even more and he heard the rushing of foaming water, knew he was above the river that cut below Duggan's high-ground hideout.

From what he had glimpsed of it on the way in here, he had seen lots of white water, which meant plenty of rocks to cause all that turbulence.

He was unable to stop his momentum,

fingers clawing up turf in their desperate bid to brake his spinning body.

Then he was falling through space and he glimpsed the raging torrent below rising to meet him.

Next, there was only thunder rumbling in his head, water gushing up his nose and filling his mouth — and lungs — as his body went down — down — down — until his boots jarred against a rocky bottom. He was flung about by the wild currents as if his limbs were being torn out by the roots.

All the air was crushed out of his lungs.

⋆　⋆　⋆

Blake stood with smoking rifle on the ledge and looked around as three men came awkwardly down the slope. Riley Duggan was one of them, his pale face reflecting the towering rage within him.

'God-*damn*! The bastard's beat us! We can say goodbye to that twelve grand now!'

Blake, face grim, angry, too, that he had been unable to kill Rand himself, said, 'Soon's it's properly light, I'll take a coupla men and check the riverbanks.'

'The hell for? You want to bury the son of a bitch?'

Blake hesitated briefly. 'No-ooo, Rile. But I want to make sure he damn well is dead.'

Duggan nodded. 'OK. But don't take too long. He's dead already I reckon. Just let me see his body.'

* * *

Darkness and violence. Choking, heart-crushing violence.

Must be the road to hell. That was his one clear thought as he was tossed and rolled, battered and beaten, over rocks and long-submerged deadfall limbs. A splintered one, the broken shards now set like knives, tore his shirt to shreds and pain seared across his torso.

No light. Only a sensation of changing hues, blurred, spinning or streaking, depending on how the currents tore at him. Consciousness began to abandon him completely now. His head was buzzing madly, his throat closed as if a maniac's hand was strangling him. His chest swelled, ready to burst at any moment. His heart was thundering like a war drum.

This was the end, then. No possible escape. He didn't even know the name of the damn river that was drowning him.

He wanted to shout in pain as his shoulder was driven against an edge of rock, then his head quickly followed and he saw cartwheeling stars, fading quickly as he plunged into the deepest and most impenetrable blackness he had ever known.

* * *

The still badly hungover outlaws staggered along the riverbanks, using the saplings Riley Duggan had ordered cut to probe into the edges of the white water, kneeling to spear the poles beneath the bank overhang where it had been undercut by long-surging waters.

Duggan had told them: 'He could be washed up and caught under them overhangs. I won't be happy till I see his body! So probe and dig and stab, wade in if you have to, but *bring me Rand's body*. Nothin' less'll satisfy me.'

The outlaws grumbled and stumbled and swore, dreaming of those first few hairs of the dog Duggan was denying them. They were in appalling condition and most didn't care whether Rand was dead or alive, or torn apart by the river and the jagged rocks. Just so they could at least find a piece of him that might satisfy Riley.

No one complained aloud too much, though. When Riley Duggan was feeling bloody, he would — and had in the past — take out his insatiable rage on anyone or anything handy.

As the morning wore on and the sun grew hotter, it became clear that they weren't going to find Rand: clear to everyone but Duggan. He swore and cursed, filling the bright morning with a mix of words and curses unsurpassed by any the searching men had ever had blistering their ears before.

His face changed from corpse-like pale to pulsing red, so dark some held their breaths, waiting for him to burst a blood vessel and drop in an apoplectic fit.

He had to sit down: his trembling legs would no longer support him and, truth was, his blood pressure was high enough to knock a crow out of a tree. He tried to roll a cigarette but his hands were too shaky, uncontrollable. Blake, clothes sodden, torn and muddy, came up, breathing hard, leaning on his stick. He dropped to the ground beside Duggan, wiped his hands on the grass, took the tobacco sack and papers from Riley's unprotesting grip.

He rolled two cigarettes, lit them both and handed one to Duggan. Both men dragged deep and exhaled lengthily.

'He's gone, Rile,' Blake said flatly. 'Gone to hell. We been over a mile downstream and wadin' through the shallows where there's no current to speak of. Not a sign of him. Well, there was his hat, some pieces of shirt like the one he'd been wearin' — and I take that as a good sign the river kinda tore him up. We can forget him, Rile.' He paused when Duggan didn't answer immediately. '*We gotta forget him!*'

'Forget him? And that twelve grand? The hell I'll forget him! This river dies to nothin' more'n a crick you can jump over come summer. We'll look again.'

Blake stared, shook his head slowly. 'You're loco. You might find a skeleton. Nothin' else.'

'Then I'll know the sonuver's dead!'

'He's dead all right, Rile. I'll bet he never even survived that drop into the white water. It woulda shot him downstream like a ball from a cannon, bouncin' off every rock in creation that was within reach.'

Riley's bleak gaze stopped Blake. 'Then why ain't you found him?'

Blake spread his aching arms. 'I

dunno. But I reckon not even a goddamn *fish* could live in that mess down there.'

'Chet Rand ain't a fish.' Duggan tossed his half-smoked cigarette away with a savage gesture, staggering to his feet. 'All right! I have to admit — he's likely dead. But after noonin', you send two of the boys downstream as far as the state line an' check every inch of the way.'

Blake nodded resignedly. 'Whatever you say, Rile.'

Duggan walked away and Blake soon followed, after glancing once more downstream, the misted river still roaring over the rapids. No one could have survived that!

No one.

8

Win or Lose

What Rand had struck his head and shoulder against was the edge of a small scooped-out hollow several feet in from the river, under the bank. It had been scoured during flood time and even now was almost full of water. But his head broke through and crashed into the roof where roots of bushes above protruded into the hollow.

It was dark, impenetrably dark. Gasping for breath, tasting an earthy mix in the back of his throat, he clung with aching fingers to a protruding rock. His legs settled to the bottom and though there was still some current it wasn't enough to bother him this far in from the mainstream.

He lay there, retching up muddy water several times, hearing the muted

133

sound of the white water in the river several feet away. He was too weak yet to do anything but stay put and, with one arm wrapped around that protruding rock, he actually slept a little.

It was the sleep of exhaustion: old instincts kept him from the normal deep torpor he might have expected. His biggest surprise when he opened his eyes was that he could see his sanctuary.

Dull, murky refracted light through the muddy water, showed him the dripping roots above, the pocked earth of the roof, the soggy walls and the sloping scoured muck that formed the bottom.

After a while he decided it meant the sun was up now, no doubt shining in full glory outside. His feet could touch bottom easily and, crawling through the shallows, he found the entrance. He held himself tense against the slight current by pressing his hands and elbows against the walls. Near the entrance he could feel the increasing tug of the river water. He panicked momentarily as it swept his feet from under him and he found himself on his back, then submerged, sucked towards the wildness beyond the bank overhang. But his boots caught and he sank his fingers deep in the muddy walls, got half his face and one ear above the level of the water that covered him.

He grunted in surprise when something sliced down through the surface, coming within inches of his body. *The hell was that? Some sort of river animal?*

It happened again and this time he saw what it was: a sapling with a sharpened point, probing, searching for him. Instinctively, he shrank back, suddenly feeling as if he was trapped in a coffin while the grave was being filled in. He had to fight for mental control as the pole raked in at an angle, actually scraped down one thigh, snagging momentarily on his trousers.

Then it was withdrawn and he waited, started forward again, mighty warily now. Suddenly the pole slammed down with much more force than previously and he yelled involuntarily. He sank as he released his holds and nearly choked, thrust his face into the few inches of available air so hard he squashed his nose into the muddy ceiling. He fought and strained not to cough as the pole probed at several different angles and reached further this time, sliding across his chest and pinning him under for several terrified seconds.

Then it was yanked out with such force he knew the manipulator was angry and frustrated at his lack of success.

He worked his way back into the very rear of the cave, found as many places to grip and hold him as he could and curled up, waiting . . .

He didn't know how long he waited, but the brightness grew stronger and then began to fade a little: he figured it was afternoon outside.

And he was near frozen.

Shivering, teeth chattering, his whole body felt as if he was beneath the icy surface of a pond. He had to watch that the cold didn't literally lock up his muscles in painful cramps so he couldn't move. He would just sink and slowly drown . . . even in these few inches of water.

After all he'd been through? Like hell!

Reserves of strength he didn't know he had were called up: he beat his arms as much as he could but without stirring his sluggish blood too much. So the only thing to do was leave, get out into the river again and the sunshine, see what Duggan and his crew had done — or if they were waiting.

Rand had no recollection of leaving his underwater sanctuary. He simply found himself lying in some tall grass and low bushes on the deserted bank. The sun was warming him and he thought maybe his tattered clothes were steaming — something which might give away his position. But, rolling over on to his belly, crawling in deeper under the brush, he parted the low branches and scanned the river. There was no one in sight. But what about above on the bank, up the slope where the camp was?

He could see no one after trying several different positions. He couldn't quite see the camp from where he stood almost waist-deep in the river. The sun hurt his eyes: it was mid-afternoon, he figured. They must have searched hard and long, checking the banks and under them in the only direction his body could have been taken by the river's surge.

Of course! Their search would have been all downstream . . . and unsuccessful, thank God.

They might come back and try again, of course, but once more it would be downstream . . . had to be. The river wouldn't — couldn't — take him any other way.

So his escape route was open to him: he would travel upstream. There was plenty of brush growing right down to the bank up that way, lots of boulders for cover, too.

He had no idea where it would take him: maybe deeper into the Cherokee Strip. But as long as it was away from Duggan's crew, he didn't care.

Weak, every bone aching or creaking, he picked up a length of fallen branch and began to make his way upstream, hugging the steep banks where the current wasn't so strong, probing with the branch to test the depth of water or the soundness of the riverbed underfoot before taking each shaky step. If he could keep going until nightfall he might yet make it out of here.

It was a win or lose situation — and the stakes were the same either way:

His life.

* * *

It was lonely out here.

A vast landscape where very little

moved: snakes and lizards, sand-coloured coyotes that blended in with the land and dusty brush, an eagle cruising the high blue but finding nothing to prey upon in the heat of the day. The burrowing animals that survived out here were deep under the ground, sleeping in the cool of their homes, conserving energy for the predatory hunt when darkness fell.

Yet for all its stillness and lack of visible natural life, there was movement: a swirling dust devil chasing a blurred shape that swayed and clattered, the front eventually forming into the shape of a team of horses. A battered old stagecoach rocked and bounced behind them, but the driver dozed in his box, boots propped against the footboard, reins bunched under the gnarled hands folded across his paunch.

The team made their own pace, followed the roughly defined trail, having made this run once a week to the swing station at Lasky's waterhole, and sometimes to the Indian reserve in the hills, for the past couple of years.

At first the trail had passed by nothing more than the waterholes where the teams watered and rested before the remainder of the run down to the main trail that eventually terminated at Columbine. But this old trail, virtually deserted except for this particular scheduled run, cut briefly across one corner of the notorious Cherokee Strip, saving many miles. So a stage station was built at Lasky's. It sounded exciting to some, passing so close to outlaw territory, but there was little or no danger.

The stage never carried anything of value, leastways, nothing that anyone knew about, and the outlaws living in the Strip were too leery about leaving their sanctuary on the long chance that there just might be something worth stealing on board.

Mostly they were right, but there had been occasions when the company, Territory Stage Lines, had taken a chance and sent urgent valuables. They had only allowed the driver to show alone in his seat, as usual, but armed guards crouched inside with the blinds drawn. But that was only very infrequently; not many customers wanted to risk themselves or their valuables that way — they preferred the regular stage run; it was longer, but more comfortable and better guarded.

The yellow coach with its dark-green-and-red trim decoration, sun-bleached and mostly unseen under the thick coating of dust, rocked along with the driver, Curly Jack Canfield, snoring as his body swayed in time with the vehicle. He had had lots of practice, and could sleep deeply like this, limbs braced just right to keep from falling.

Deeply enough not to hear someone pounding on the roof with a sunshade handle from inside the coach and shouting his name.

When this produced no results one of the flapping canvas window blinds was released. It snapped a cloud of dust into the dim interior, causing the lone occupant to cough and sneeze several times.

The passenger was a woman in her mid-twenties, well dressed in a grey-and-white dress with matching gloves and a small hat of the same shades with a contrasting blue-dyed feather on the left side. Her hair was brown and caught back with a mother-of-pearl and ivory pin, showing all of her face and small pink ears.

She looked a pleasant woman, despite her annoyance at this moment, her nose maybe a little too large above a mouth just a mite too wide, so that she wouldn't be called 'beautiful' — but sure not 'ugly'! Sometimes a pleasant face went a long way, often further than a beautiful one would take its owner.

'Curly *Jack!*' she called irritably, poking her head out of the window, still ramming the ornate head of the sunshade against the roof with the one hand still inside the coach. The other clung to the outside of the dusty door and she curled her nose at the feel of the grit working its way inside her glove. 'Curly Jack *Canfield*! You answer me this instant!'

She leaned out further, the wind unsettling her hat though it still stayed attached to her hair by the ivory pin. Awkwardly she reached up with the sunshade and prodded hard. That woke Curly Jack Canfield in a hurry, so much that he swore aloud. Then, holding on to his battered old hat which was now askew on his head, he glimpsed the woman.

'Oh, my gosh, ma'am! Ah — Ah'm truly sorry for my language. Din' mean to — '

'I can abide your cussing, Jack, but I can *not* abide this endless rolling and bumping! Good heavens, man, I'm supposed to have all my books in order by the time I arrive at the station, and I cannot work on them when they are flying all around the coach and getting trampled under my feet! Can't you do something? Besides sleep, I mean.'

'Ah'm truly sorry, ma'am. It's muh

habit to doze on this here trail an' well, ah don't bring many passengers.'

She almost bounced out the window as they hit a big rut; she clutched at her hat and just saved it from flying off. Her hair began to unravel and she started to withdraw into the coach interior.

'Do something now, if you please! Right now!'

She sagged back on to her seat, one hand still holding to the window sill, tried to push hair out of her eyes where it was now tumbling over her face. Then her education was given another boost as Curly Jack laid into the team, cracking his whip, standing on the seat as he manipulated the reins, actually steering the flying horses around and between ruts and dips and potholes.

It wasn't a great improvement but a lot better than it had been. The girl pinned her hair back swiftly and got down on her knees between the seats, picking up her papers and notebooks, muttering a mild swear word herself when she saw that every one of her six pencils had broken their points during the rough ride.

'Oh, I must have been crazy to volunteer to come this way! Absolutely — crazy . . . Oh! *Oh!*'

Abruptly, she was thrown across her pile of books and they scattered again as the stage suddenly slithered and swerved madly, shuddered violently with a cacophony of creaks and snaps and the screech of metal against metal; the smell of burning leather brake-blocks wafted through the window.

She ended up with one leg on the seat, the skirt of her dress somewhere in the region of her waist, frilled pants legs not only showing, but *torn* on a screw head that was part of the seat.

Now this was too much! But even as she struggled to pull herself up on to the seat, she realized the stage had stopped completely. Curly Jack, once again apparently oblivious to the tender ears of his passenger, was cutting loose with a tirade of a trail driver's inventory of endearments usually specifically reserved for misbehaving cattle.

She blinked at such blistering language, fascinated by the inventiveness as much as appalled by its being rendered within her hearing.

But, curious, she made her way across to the door, trampling her notes and books, fought the worn brass handle and stepped down. She almost fell, as the stage was slightly tilted in a dip in the trail and she had chosen the high side to dismount from.

'What — what's happened?'

Jack swallowed and cleared his throat, towering above her on the canted roof of the coach. He pointed with his curled whip. 'Yonder!'

She shaded her eyes, still having to squint in the bright sun. A frown briefly embossed her smooth forehead.

'You mean that . . . what is it? Something lying in the trail?'

'That somethin' is a man — or what's left of him!' Jack told her. He lifted the lid of the seat box and fumbled out the sawn-off shotgun, these days beginning, for some reason, to be referred to as a 'coach' gun in correspondence from Head Office in Denver.

'What're you doing?'

Clambering down carefully, holding the gun out to one side, Jack, paused as he reached the ground, wheezing; he was a heavy smoker and, she suspected, a heavy drinker as well, not in very good shape.

'If he's playin' possum, I'll need this.' He patted the dusty blued barrels of the gun.

'He's not moving. He might be hurt.'

Jack turned his head and spat, nodding gently.

'That's likely. Seen his clothes from high up. Looks like an old scarecrow's, tattered, half ripped off.' He gave her a sharp look. 'Mebbe you better wait here. I mean, if his trousers are . . . '

She flushed. 'I have attended injured men in all stages of dress and undress, Curly Jack Canfield, as you well know. We'll have to take him with us if he's hurt, won't we?'

He hesitated, then nodded. 'That's the usual thing.'

'Well, why are we wasting time, talking about it?'

She started towards the body of the man ten yards along the trail, able to see him a little more clearly now. He was half-buried in dust and she guessed he had been lying there for quite some time. She turned towards the wheezing driver.

'Well, get a move on, can't you? He could be dying.'

'More'n likely already dead if he's been lyin' in this heat for long. OK, let's go see.'

9

Resurrection

It was so dark and quiet, he thought he was still trapped under the riverbank. But then there had been some movement: small ripples, a hand-span swirl, sucking sounds when the water lapped the low entrance.

Nothing like that now.

The smell! Other senses besides his hearing and sight cut in and he realized he could not smell the dank mustiness or the stench of the mud. Touch was next: he could move his arms and legs but no water enveloped them, though something did — something light, yet resilient, like . . . cloth?

With a grunt he sat up, grunted again, but this time in brief pain as stiff, aching muscles were called into action. His hands pressed against something soft and he bunched up what could only have been a bed cover. Before it became a conscious thought, he knew he was in bed, somewhere — but *how* had he come here?

He sat very still, a faint whistling and a bubbling in his left ear: waterlogged. He canted his head, used the heel of his right hand to pound his skull above his ear on that side and felt the warm liquid flow from his left, downward-pointing ear as he dislodged residual water.

'Part of the damn river!' He stiffened at how raspy and harsh his voice sounded, how it hurt his throat which, he realized, now ached and felt raw and inflamed. His eyes were gritty, and there was a light bandage around his head and one shoulder!

He sat there, body rigid, hands bunching the bed covers, memory beginning to come back.

The escape from Riley Duggan's gang; dynamite; the goddamned river and the plunge down the white-water rapids . . .

It was all coming back: the freezing hours trapped below the riverbank. The plunging, probing, sharpened saplings reaching for his body . . . *a gap*, then making his way out into fresh air and sunshine, figuring out that his best bet lay in working his way *up*stream. Then groping, stumbling, staggering along the edge of the river, occasionally the current sweeping his legs from under him and all the while the frantic spluttering, grabbing at rocks or a bush, anything anchored firmly in the bank.

Another gap in his memory: it seemed a long, long gap, then — a butte towering above him — the rear of the one where Duggan had his hideout — far enough inland now so he could neither see nor hear the distant river.

A roly-poly descent down slopes of stunted grass, pain, flailing limbs. Once more staggering along more or less upright — *less*, if you want to remember it right. Crawling, thirst — with a whole damn river somewhere behind! But nothing known in front.

Suddenly aware it was dark, lifting his face out of gravel, crawling in the coolness of night — crawling — still crawling, hands bleeding, knees raw, clothes in rags from snagging brush and stones, his flesh scratched . . .

Sun half-blinding him as he opened his eyes and found he was on a low ledge on a slope, back propped against a gritty boulder. Too exhausted to even keep his eyes open, he let the lead-heavy lids shut down of their own accord.

An instant later — *was it really so soon?* — he opened them and squinted, hearing before seeing. What he heard was a distant rattle and thumping. Using his fingers to hold his eyelids apart he saw the dust cloud, away to his right, lifting from what looked like . . . like a trail. Sunlight flashed from yellow as the vehicle rounded a curve. He saw the movement of the driver, whip snaking over a thundering team.

He started up involuntarily, a choking, unintelligible cry forcing itself over his parched lips.

But he moved too fast, too clumsily, stepped right off his ledge and tumbled and skidded and rolled and finally somersaulted on to dusty ground that must be a part of the trail itself. But he lost consciousness before the thought reached his brain.

Now — *now* — he was in a bed — somewhere — and someone had obviously tended to his wounds. He tried to call out but his throat closed. He tried clearing it, making sounds like an animal in distress. It started a fit of coughing, and before it was over a thin band of light streaked beneath a door. The door opened, and a woman, wearing a hastily-donned robe over her nightgown, hurried in, carrying a lamp which she set on a box on the floor near his bed.

Tender, soft hands soothed his hot brow and his eyes moved in their sockets as she turned his head this way and that, examining it in the dim orange light cast by the lamp.

'You've knocked the scabs off a few scratches, but only one is actually bleeding,' she told him and he saw the comforting smile as she eased him back on the pillow. 'Just rest. You're safe here.'

He managed one word. 'H-here . . . ?'

'Lasky's Waterhole — the stageline swing station. We picked you up a long way back down the trail. You were in pretty bad shape but you're coming along nicely now.'

'H-how — long?'

'How long have you been here? This will be the fourth day, just starting. And a fine day it's going to be, too. Not a cloud to be seen and just a light zephyr blowing out of the north, so it should keep things comfortably cool.'

He lifted a hand revealing his scratched and gnarled fingers; his lips were working. Her smile broadened as she drew a sheet up across his chest.

'I think you're trying to thank me. Don't worry. Just to see you starting to come good is thanks enough. I'm Georgia Horan by the way. My uncle owns Territory Stagelines and I'm helping him out with some of his bookwork. Can you tell me who you are?' she added swiftly, when she saw him frown. 'If you don't wish to, that's all right, I'll just call you — let me see . . . how about 'Moses'? He had experience with a river, too.' Then she laughed briefly at the way he blinked and stared at her. She patted his face. 'No, I'm not a witch! You talked a good deal when you were semi-conscious and kept mentioning a river where you almost drowned.'

He nodded, looked a little relieved. As she turned towards the door, smiling, thoughtfully leaving the lamp burning on the box, he rasped:

'Ch-Chet — Rand.'

She paused, sombre now, staring at him and making him feel uncomfortable. Then the smile was back and she nodded.

'Yes — a more fitting name than 'Moses', I'm sure. Rest now. I'll look in again later.'

* * *

Todd Reason was the swing station manager and he was not happy that the boss's niece had moved in and was going through the books: books he was supposed to keep up to date, and which were a long way out of date and far from accurate.

He was an ordinary-looking ranny, until you noticed the eyes, closer-set than was usual, not only narrowed, but dark, so dark there didn't seem to be any pupils. Or maybe the eyes were *all* pupils, which could not be the case. He hadn't shaved in a few days and stood now at the foot of the porch steps, running work-hardened fingers over the stubble with a rasping sound as he stared up at Georgia.

She stood on the porch holding two ragged books in her hands, one opened. She tapped the blotched ink words with a finger.

'You're not a very good bookkeeper, Todd.'

'I ain't s'posed to be,' he told her, surly and annoyed, knowing what her close inspection would eventually uncover. 'I do a hard day's work, breakin' in knot-headed broncs ready to go into change-over teams, wear myself out tryin' to get a day's work outta them 'breed roustabouts, and when I come in for supper, I'm plumb tuckered. Knowin' I gotta wrassle pages of damn figures after I've et don't entice me at all.'

She stiffened at his tone. 'It's part of your job, Todd, and you know it. But it's not just that you've neglected to keep the books up to date, I'm a professional book-keeper and I can detect poorly disguised discrepancies here that can only mean one thing.'

She paused and his mean eyes narrowed as he rested one hand on his hip. 'Yeah? An' what's that?'

'That you've been short-changing the stores for the reservation — and, I would suspect, selling back to them at an enormous profit, as well as others

— I suppose they have to be men from the Cherokee Strip. It's only a few miles away.'

His mouth tightened. 'You can't prove nothin'.'

'Not right this minute, Todd, but your attempt at covering up is very transparent. You know it amounts to stealing from the company? Not to mention the Territorial Government.'

He didn't answer right away, stared hard, and she felt a queasiness in her belly when those bad eyes settled on her.

'Mebbe if your skinflint uncle paid me a decent wage, I wouldn't have to try an' make a little extra.'

'From what I've heard, if you stayed away from the Indian women and the moonshiners, you wouldn't need any extra.'

'Where you hear that? Damn Curly Jack, I bet! He's always pokin' his nose in where it ain't wanted. I warned him I'd bust it for him, tweak it right off his stupid face — '

159

'Todd, I think we'll end this here. I haven't yet figured out how much you've stolen but I'm willing to let it stand in lieu of paying you what wages you're owed.'

'*What*? Judas, who the hell you think you are?'

She gave a cry of alarm and dropped the account books as he leapt up on to the porch. She turned to the door but he grabbed her ponytail and she cried aloud in pain and terror as he yanked her back so hard and fast that her feet tangled and she lost balance, fell sprawling on her back.

'You interferin' bitch! I'll teach you to come out here with your uppitty ways and . . . '

He still held her hair and she put up her hands, trying to ease the pressure as she felt her scalp stretching painfully. She was kicking wildly and making half-crying, half-angry sounds.

Then there was a brain-jarring slap as he leaned over and struck her across the face.

She gasped rather than cried out, then suddenly he released her hair and she watched in amazement as Todd Reason stumbled to his knees, hands clutching his head.

A pair of denim-clad legs came into the orbit of her vision and she glanced up through welling tears of pain as Chet Rand drove a boot against Reason's spine and sent the man tumbling out into the yard, where he floundered, dazed.

Rand reached down and grabbed Georgia's arm, hauling her to her feet. He grunted and winced with the effort and she saw that the heavy carved walking-stick which some passenger had left behind and which had been on a narrow shelf just inside the door, was now in Rand's free hand. She guessed this was what he had hit Reason with before kicking him off the porch.

'Best go inside,' he told her without looking at her, watching Reason stagger to his feet.

Todd's face was gravel-scarred from

his fall and his eyes blazed with fury as he glared at Rand. He reached for his six-gun, mouthing threats and curses. Rand lunged forward and threw the heavy walking stick. It whistled through the air and cracked against Reason's gun arm, above the elbow. He yelled and spun away. Rand picked up the stick and slammed it across the back of Reason's head. He fell to his knees, face in his hands, swaying, barely conscious. Chet Rand placed a boot against his chest, pushed him back to the ground and stood towering over the man, keeping pressure on the boot.

'Get your gear and light out. If you're still here in thirty minutes I'll kill you.'

As he spoke Rand reached down, unbuckled the man's six-gun rig and wrenched it out from under him, half rolling his body. Holding the gun rig in one hand, the heavy stick in the other, Rand waited, giving Reason time to get his senses in order.

The man got to his feet, staggered and swayed, holding his head, a red snake of blood crawling down from under his hairline.

'You — you got no call to — buy into this!'

'Just get your gear and go, mister.'

In a few seconds Rand had the gun rig buckled around his own waist. Reason's eyes widened as the Colt appeared in his fist almost magically. He closed his mouth and turned to hurry towards the corrals when Rand cocked the hammer.

Georgia stepped down beside him. 'Thank you, but . . . I didn't think you were strong enough for — '

He gave her a crooked smile. 'I'm not. Feel like I'm half-floating and you should be hearing my knees knocking together any minute now.'

She steadied him, urged him back into the house.

'Not till he goes. Don't let him see how weak I am.'

'You've only been walking around for less than a day!'

'That all? Feels like I climbed that

knoll and ran all the way back. Twice.'

They watched while Todd Reason tied his warbag behind the saddle he had thrown on to a big sorrel. He looked at the rifle in its scabbard for a moment, flicked his gaze to where Rand still stood holding the cocked six-gun, then mounted.

He spurred out of the yard, riding close enough to send stones and dust scattering towards the woman and Rand.

'I'll see you again, mister!' Reason shouted.

'Look forward to it!' Rand called back. Then his legs started to fold, so the girl took him to the awning post and he leaned against it, clinging tightly with one hand until Reason was out of sight.

'He's a vindictive man, Chet. You'll need to watch out if ever you meet him again.'

He grunted. 'Might have a — bit of a lie down,' he slurred and almost collapsed.

She somehow managed to get him into his room where he flopped across the bed.

He still held the Colt, though he had lowered the hammer.

★ ★ ★

Another couple of days made a big difference in Chet Rand. It wasn't just the rest and the changing of the bandages over his wounds, nor even the good food that Georgia cooked.

Much of his improvement was due to the girl's company.

She was bright and compassionate, knowledgeable, and he knew she must be glad of his company. Now that Reason had left, there were only the 'breed roustabouts from the reservation living down in their own small encampment a quarter-mile from the main building.

Stages were few and the driver was usually Curly Jack Canfield or one of his fellow-drivers: they were all taciturn men. Mind, they knew their job, were experts in desert crossings with over-loaded stages, and wilderness survival; he figured they were mostly uncomfort-able with having to deal with a woman as 'boss'.

'I learned a lot from such men in other out-of-the-way stage stations,' she told Rand over supper on the second night after she had fired Reason. 'I find it interesting but because I'm 'the boss's' niece, I think I sort of intimidate them.' She paused, looked at him over the rim of her coffee cup and smiled as she added, 'I'm very glad I don't intimidate you, Chet.'

'Don't find you intimidating. Just the opposite. I'm mighty grateful to you for saving me. No, you saved my life. I could've easily died out there on that trail. If you hadn't taken me in — '

'Oh, Jack Canfield would never have left you lying there.'

He gave her a half-smile. 'He's not as good-looking as you.' She didn't blush but gave him a steady stare and he saw she was pleased at the compliment. 'You know how to tend injuries.'

There was a question there and she told him how, when she first decided to come out West, she had studied nursing procedures and had a cousin who was a doctor and who had helped her.

'I thought such knowledge might prove useful.'

'It was useful to me.'

'I'm glad, Chet. But never mind about me. How well are you feeling now?'

'Just about fit enough to ride.'

'Don't be silly. You'll need at least another week to fully recover. In any case, I wasn't asking because of that.'

'No? Well, I won't bother you for much longer just the same. That's if you can let me have a mount. And maybe a rifle. I feel kind of naked without a Winchester handy.'

Her grey eyes were steady. 'Guns are an important part of your life?'

'Sure. You run a horse ranch that depends on mustangs for stock, it's gotta be well away from what passes for civilization. Which means you have to hunt your meat, protect yourself — from wild men as well as wild animals.'

'Of course. I don't know that part of Colorado where you said you came from — Rattle Creek? Yet I seem to have heard of it not too long ago. Perhaps my uncle mentioned it or it appeared on one of the many survey maps he's commissioned.'

'What's he surveying?'

'Oh, he's always looking for areas where he can expand the stageline. He's very rich and has road engineers and land agents on permanent call all over the frontier.'

'When I get back to Columbine, you want I should send him a wire and tell him you need a new manager out here? And mebbe an extra white man or two instead of having to be alone with 'breeds?'

A little stiffly, she told him, 'I find I get along well enough with ' 'breeds' as you call them, even the full bloods. I've worked with Commanches, Kiowa, and even Jicarilla Apaches.'

'That reservation yonder is for Mescalero Apaches. Can't always trust 'em. Though it depends on the individual.'

'Just the same as with white men!'

He smiled, sensing this was a touchy subject with her. 'Yeah, just like that,' he agreed readily. 'Mebbe you could ask for a married wrangler or manager? Give you a little feminine company.'

She lightened up and gave him a slight curtsy as they stood. 'Thank you for thinking of my welfare. But, please, don't leave too soon. Apart from endangering your health I-I enjoy your company.'

'I'll stick around a few days. I'm not quite as chipper as I try to make out,' he confessed a mite ruefully. 'And just in case Reason decides to come back.'

Alarm washed swiftly over her face. 'He won't — will he?'

'Might — if I'm still here. He had the look of a man who won't forget a hurt and I made a fool of him in front of you.'

'But I'm only one person! It's not as if there were half a dozen witnesses — '

'One's too many for scum like Reason.' He realized he might be frightening her so changed the subject again. 'Can I pick a mount from your remuda? And maybe select one of them rifles you've got? Not sure when I'll be able to pay you back but I will.'

'Be my guest.'

He grinned. 'Already am — and I won't forget it.'

She flushed but felt a surge of pleasure for she knew he meant what he said.

Then, hesitantly, as she began to clear away the supper things, she said, 'I don't suppose you'd consider . . . taking over Reason's job? Even if it was only for a few weeks until you've fully recovered . . . ?'

He regarded her soberly. 'It's tempting, Georgia. But there are a few things I have to do. Maybe I could come back this way if I get 'em settled, could wait until you get a replacement . . . '

Her face truly beamed. She might be able to persuade him to stay on permanently . . .

'Now that is the best idea I've heard in a long time!'

He was surprised when he felt himself flushing.

10

The Columbine Trail

A few days later Rand rode away from the swing station on the buckskin he had chosen from Georgia's remuda, a Winchester rifle in .44/.40 calibre in the saddle scabbard, Reason's Colt on his right hip.

He was a little uneasy about leaving Georgia but there was one of the Indians, a middle-aged man who had spent time in a white mission, who seemed protective of her. He was called Quiet Dog by the others and obviously had some standing with them.

'I helped deliver one of his sons last time I was out this way and his young wife had a difficult birth,' Georgia told Rand. 'I'll be alright.'

'Yeah. Indians don't forget good

turns like that. I feel better about leaving now.'

She smiled. 'You're a thoughtful man, Chet Rand.'

He smiled back. 'I don't forget good turns, either.'

She was a confident woman and, to help his peace of mind, demonstrated that she could use a rifle as well as most men, shooting stones off the top rail of an empty corral at a distance of thirty yards.

'Well, if anyone hostile gets closer to you than that, he's a goner!' Rand commented and he heard her full, genuine responsive laugh for the first time.

As he paused on the ridge, looked back and waved at her small figure watching him from her porch, he was still hearing that pleasant laughter echoing in his mind.

Yeah — he'd make a special point of coming back this way . . .

But Todd Reason had other ideas.

The surly, crooked station manager

could not forget how a wounded man had beaten him and kicked him off the stageline land. He had seen some of the 'breed roustabouts watching and he knew they would spread the word about how he had been forced to leave like a whipped cur.

He had thought of holing up on one of the ridges near the station and picking off a few of those damn 'breeds just for the hell of it. Then he figured a better idea would be to pick off Rand.

But underlying his simmering rage, there was a hollowness in his belly: even though he had been beaten and fresh out of sick bed, there was something about Chet Rand that twanged a taut nerve in Reason.

No — a better idea would be to lie in wait along the trail.

That was what Todd Reason did.

As Rand came over a rise, a steep slope falling away so that he had to concentrate on the buckskin, Reason sighted down his rifle barrel from where he lay in the shade of a tall needle rock.

The rock was narrow, and the shade had shifted almost imperceptibly as the sun rose higher. Reason didn't realize that when he lifted the rifle, half the length of the barrel was in full sunlight. He was concentrating on setting his sights squarely on Rand's chest and wasn't aware of the sun-flash off the blued metal.

Rand, holding the reins taut as the buckskin started down the steep incline, caught the edge of that burst of light, snapped his head up in time to see it. He wrenched the reins sharply left, causing the horse to leap almost behind a jutting boulder.

An instant later, Reason's bullet whined off the same rock, dust and chips, flying. Still feeling some stiffness, Rand dropped out of leather, pulled the startled horse in closer to the rock and slid the Winchester from the scabbard. He crouched as three more hasty shots raked the boulder. He smiled crookedly as Reason shouted in frustrated anger, 'Goddamn you, you lousy bounty hunter!'

Rand kicked a head-sized rock over the ends of the trailing reins, slid around and worked his way beneath two boulders leaning against each other. He saw the powder smoke rising above Reason's hiding place — there was not enough breeze yet to disperse it. He levered, held his sights below the gunsmoke, and waited.

There was nothing subtle about Todd Reason. His reactions were those of a primitive man: instant rage, which smothered intelligent reaction or thought. He shifted position immediately after loosing his volley, trying to get to a better site in the untidy pile of rocks near the base of the needle. Chet put two fast shots into Reason's cover, the bullets ricocheting from the closely packed rocks, not just once, but because of the nearness of the rockfaces, three or four times, each with a snarling, howling intensity.

Reason fell, yelling a curse. His rifle clattered as it dropped into a crevice and, in panic, he hurled himself down, crawled under the boulders and rolled out into the space where he had left his mount. Unarmed now and with fear churning within him, he fumbled his leap at the saddle, half-slid across, one boot only in the stirrup, and yelled into the startled horse's ear. It charged out of the rocks and when it appeared, Rand stood up, drew aim, then changed his mind, angled the rifle barrel towards the sky and triggered two fast shots.

Reason flopped into the saddle properly, somehow managed to grab his reins and got the hell out of there as fast as the horse could take him.

Rand watched for a few minutes until the man disappeared into the depths of the boulder field. He was going away from the direction of the swing station and Rand figured he wouldn't come back and give Georgia any trouble.

Besides, unarmed now, Todd Reason would be thinking only of his own safety.

★ ★ ★

'Hey, Riley! Lookit what I got here!'

Riley Duggan glanced up irritably at the call. It was one of the guards from the high trail that led to the outlaw hideout. Duggan was busy sketching a planned hold-up of the regular stage on the Columbine run: one of his paid informants had gotten word to him that the stage would be carrying money on transfer to the First Territorial Bank. Still smarting that he had missed out on getting his hands on the $12,000 payroll that Feeney had grabbed, Riley aimed to make this hold-up a success, hell or high water.

Blake was with him, holding a torn and greasy wrinkled geological survey map that included the stage route. He jumped to his feet as the guard came riding in, dragging a man at the end of his rope.

'Looks like Todd Reason!'

Riley frowned and stood as the the guard hauled rein. Reason, dusty and gagging, clothes torn, rolled several times to within a few feet of Riley and

Blake. Other outlaws lounging around the hideaway showed little interest: Reason was no one to get excited about, just a petty thief who stole goods from the swing station and sold them to the outlaws at exorbitant prices. No one had much respect for him.

'He was comin' likety-split up our trail, Rile,' the guard said, flicking his rope free as Reason staggered upright and fumbled his way out of the loop. 'Figured the devil hisself was after him but it's only that damn bounty hunter threw a scare into him, he says.'

Duggan stiffened. 'Which bounty hunter?'

'That one we thought'd drowned in the river,' the guard answered and started as Riley lunged past the mount and grabbed the wide-eyed Reason.

He shook the man roughly. 'Goddamn you, Reason, *who we talkin' about?* Chet Rand?'

Reason nodded vigorously, afraid of Riley Duggan. In fact, any visit here to the outlaw hideout always made him kind of sick to his stomach. These were rough men and sometimes he wished he'd never started dealing with them. He made a good profit but it cost him plenty in nervous tension.

He was mighty nervous now as he haltingly explained to Duggan and Blake about Rand, how he had been brought to the swing station and nursed back to health by Georgia Horan.

'I *told* you that bastard wasn't dead!' Riley Duggan snarled to no one in particular. 'I said I wouldn't b'lieve it until I saw his body!' He spun on his heel as the rage surged through him, then swept off his hat and slammed it into the dust. 'Judas *Priest*! Where the hell is he now?'

This last was flung at Reason who stepped back hurriedly. 'Left him along the Columbine trail — just past the Needle . . . '

'He follow you?' snapped Blake.

Reason shook his head. 'I-I dunno for sure. I just got outta there fast. Riley, you gotta let me stay here a spell. He'll kill me if he catches up.'

Duggan glared and suddenly smiled: he had found a target to help rid himself of the towering rage that possessed him. 'Sure, Todd. You can stay. Permanent.'

His six-gun came up and he shot Reason three times, startling both Blake and the guard.

'Loudmouth would've given away this place sooner or later. Get him buried or drop him down a hole. Blake, you and me are ridin'.'

*   *   *

Rand saw them coming as he topped out on a ridge, late in the afternoon.

He had paused to roll a cigarette, dismounting, allowing the horse to crop a small patch of grass. He was stiff and aching, the abused muscles and tendons from his time in the river were not yet fully healed, and not helped any by this long ride.

The match flare as he lit up blinded

him briefly. Then he saw the dust cloud below, on the flats he had recently ridden across. Cigarette dangling from his lips, he stood, adjusting the brim of the hat Georgia had found for him, so his eyes were shaded.

Two riders. Coming fast, following his trail, already closing in on the base of the ridge below. They must have seen him, for he hadn't been trying to hide after Reason had vamoosed, unarmed and showing his yellow streak.

But neither of these riders was Todd Reason, and yet, there was something familiar . . .

'Riley Duggan and Blake!' he said aloud, dropping the cigarette and grinding it out under foot.

He startled the buckskin with the way he slammed against its side as he slid the Winchester from the scabbard. He swiftly levered a cartridge into the breech, slapped the mount on the rump so that it whinnied briefly, then moved a few yards away, but turned its head with a kind of challenging look as it bent to the grass once more.

Rand vaulted a deadfall, fell awkwardly and dropped the rifle. He flung himself after it, crawled back swiftly to settle into a defensive position.

There was no sign of the outlaws, except for a rapidly dispersing dust cloud where they had ridden into cover. The slopes were studded with boulders and numerous deadfalls but he figured they would have made for the narrow cutting at the base. They could leave the mounts there and make their way up on foot. If he ran for his horse and mounted, he would be silhouetted for too long before he could drop over the crest out of sight, and even then, one of them might be in a position to pick him off from that side.

This was outlaw territory: Duggan and Blake would know it as well as they knew their own names.

A rifle cracked twice from below and two bullets tore splinters from his deadfall, a couple of feet to the left of his position; it was damned good shooting at that angle and range.

It surprised him to realize that the rifleman must be so far up the slope; likely they knew shortcuts, and it only drove home how much he was disadvantaged here.

He figured they would want to take him alive — which was no comfort: he'd already experienced their 'hospitality'. This time it would be a lot worse than previously: Riley Duggan would still be convinced he knew where the $12,000 was.

So, he had to shoot to kill. They might want to talk to him, but there was no conversation he needed with those two.

He crawled along to the left behind the deadfall, figuring the man who had shot at him would compensate and move his gun to the right. A few seconds later he was proved correct as several bullets chewed flying slivers from the top of the fallen tree. He was above a slight hollow in the ground that the deadfall straddled. He dropped to his belly and slid into the depression, able to peer beneath the log, and see a wide area of slope.

He glimpsed a red shirt as a man below moved to better cover or a better position to shoot from. Rand let his gaze run ahead, spotted the narrow gap in the rocks down there which he figured the man was making for.

Yes! There was that flash of red as he slid into position. Rand triggered, levered, but held fire on the second shot. He heard the brief scream and the man in the red shirt reared up, hands clawing at his bloody face before he pitched forward and hung up in the rocks, an arm dangling, blood dripping and smearing the ground. His hat fell off revealing the unkempt dark curls of Riley Duggan.

Then a bullet slammed into the log beside him with a solid *thunk*! Instinct made him drop lower and he slid under the log and through to the far side.

That shot had come from behind him, which meant that Blake had somehow gotten above him. More lead raked the log; if there hadn't been that hollow beneath he would be dead by now.

He slipped, sliding away from the deadfall, far enough apparently to reveal him to the killer. The ground around him spurted in three small but violent eruptions of stones and stinging dirt. He threw himself backwards, landing on his shoulders, started to slide.

Realizing he had lost the protection of the deadfall, he tried to twist around in an effort to stop his descent. He glimpsed the killer on his feet now, rifle to shoulder, taking his aim confidently.

Rand brought his own rifle across his body one-handed and triggered. It was about as wild a shot as he had ever made and the lead struck a flat-sided rock six feet to Blake's right. It sounded like an angry hornet. The flattened lead must have passed close to the outlaw, for he jerked, lost his footing and fell, rolling out of sight. By then Rand had managed to turn his body so that he lay across the slope. It slowed him and he swiftly dug in the rifle in an effort to stop his slide.

It filled the barrel with packed dirt and grit, but as soon as he stopped he tossed the now useless Winchester aside, reached for his six-gun and flung himself back towards the shelter of the deadfall. He was now on the downslope side.

Blake must have had a bad fright from that ricochet. Rand heard him running and vaulted the log, pounding up the slope in pursuit. He skidded around some rocks at the top, was in time to see Blake, one arm bloody and dangling, running along the edge of the steep drop behind the ridge. He saw Rand and fired a shot with his Colt; he must have lost his rifle when the ricochet slashed his arm.

Rand, still running, shoulder-rolled as Blake continued to fire in a panic. He came up on one knee, grabbed his right wrist with his left hand and tracked Blake's wildly weaving figure before dropping the hammer. The Colt still bucked, even with the two-handed grip, but the bullet sped true.

It picked up Blake and flung him over the edge.

Rand didn't bother going to look: it was over a hundred feet straight down.

11

Return

It was almost sundown when Rand rode into Columbine, and dismounted at the hitch rail outside the telegraph office. He draped the reins of the weary buckskin over the rail, but tied the lead rope of the second horse, which carried Riley Duggan's body, securely.

Inside, he handed Georgia's message for her uncle in Denver to the telegraphist, who took it without glancing up from a paper he was reading. There was a ten-dollar coin wrapped in the page she had written on and the man said it would be enough to pay for the wire.

Rand walked both horses down Springer Street, folk on the boardwalks stopping to stare at the blanket-draped figure on the second horse. A few people followed, but at a wary distance.

There was a light burning in the law office when he tied both horses to the hitch rail. The murmur of the small crowd must have made Brock Powers curious for he appeared in the doorway, hatless, vest unbuttoned, a cigarette in his left hand, and not wearing his gun rig. He stopped when he saw Rand uncovering the dead man.

'Who the hell is that?' The lawman leapt down from the landing and yanked the dead man's head up by the hair. When he saw the bloody ruin of the face, he swore, lifted a bleak gaze to Rand's trail-dusted face. 'I repeat: *who the hell is that*?'

'Riley Duggan.'

Powers snorted. 'The hell you say! It could be Santa Claus, far as anyone can tell. Christ! How'd he get smashed up like that?'

'Ricochet.'

'Yours, I s'pose?'

'He and an outlaw named Blake tried to kill me. Blake went over a cliff — this was in The Strip, out of your jurisdiction.' Rand's gaze steadied on Powers' face. 'Figured there ought to be a bounty on Duggan so I brought him in.'

'There's a bounty — more'n one — on Riley Duggan.' Powers stepped back and pointed to the draped corpse. 'But that sure don't look like him to me.'

Powers glanced at the crowd. There were some murmurings, but no one spoke up and said straight out that they thought the dead man was Riley.

Rand sighed. 'You gonna block my claim to this one, too, like you did with Feeney?'

Powers shrugged. 'You prove to me it's Duggan and I'll look into it.' The sheriff grinned tightly. 'Ought to place your bullets more careful so's your victims can be identified easy if you want to collect any bounty.'

Powers was enjoying frustrating Rand but showed a little wariness at the glint of simmering anger in the bounty hunter's eyes.

'Take a look at one of the wanted dodgers — see if it mentions any identifying scars or something.'

Powers shook his head. 'They don't.'

'Your memory must be pretty damn good!'

'Mister, Duggan has been a wanted man for years in this Territory. I can quote you every dodger put out on him.'

Rand knew he wasn't going to get anywhere. He suddenly tossed the lead rope at Powers and the sheriff, startled, instinctively caught it. By that time, Rand was mounting the buckskin again.

'Hey! Where you think you're goin'?'

'First to the livery, then likely to the saloon. I got a lousy taste in my mouth I need to wash away.'

'You take this corpse down to the undertaker's before you do anythin', and then you come in my office and make a statement.'

Rand was already turning the buckskin away from the hitch rack. 'Later.'

'Goddamnit! You'll do it when I say!'

'Would, if you'd agreed that's Riley Duggan. I'll be back, Sheriff.'

The sheriff could have run into his office and grabbed a gun, he even started to, but he caught the now mostly hostile faces of the crowd. And someone said quite clearly,

'You ask me that's Riley Duggan. Know him by the curly hair and his build. Always liked red shirts, too.'

A couple of others agreed quietly, looking warily at the lawman. But all Powers could do now, after growling, 'Well, *I* ain't satisfied!' was watch, simmering, as Rand turned his horse down the street towards Chapman's livery.

The stable man seem friendlier than the last time Rand was here. He stood packing a pipe outside the stall as he watched Rand off-saddle the weary buckskin gelding.

'Recognize that TSL brand: Territory Stageline, ain't it?'

'They lent it to me out at Lasky's.'

'We wondered where you'd got to.'

Puffing smoke as he got his pipe drawing, Chapman continued to watch as Rand unsheathed his rifle: he had taken time to clear the barrel of the dirt before leaving the ridge where he had shot it out with Duggan and Blake, let running water in a small creek flush the barrel through. He would need to oil it as soon as possible to prevent rust build-up.

Rand picked up his warbag, turned to the other man. 'Not exactly plush for money right now. OK if I sleep in your loft tonight?'

'Cost you half a dollar, includin' the stall. You wanna pay now?'

Rand smiled thinly, digging in his pocket for a coin: Georgia had given him a little money to see him through. 'Making sure you get what's due, huh?'

'We-ell. You look like a thirsty man to me.' At Rand's puzzled look, Chapman said, 'Lew, the barkeep, and Jerry Halstead've both been mouthin'-off about you since they got back — lookin' the worse for wear. Which they blame you for ... specially Jerry.'

Rand nodded slowly, handing over his half-dollar. 'If I had more to spare, reckon I'd give you a tip.'

'I'll give you one instead. Go into the saloon by the side door on the north side — not the south door. That opens straight into the corner where Jerry's set himself up at a table. Lew's keepin' him supplied with likker. I think they're kinda hopin' you'll go in for a drink.'

'Obliged, mister.' As Rand started to move away the stableman said,

'Hear you stuck up for The Duke earlier. You know he's in Doc Swanson's infirmary?'

Rand stiffened. 'I hadn't heard. Pneumonia again?'

'You know better'n that. Sheriff brought him in, all bloodied and beat up. Says he found him that way on the bank of the creek behind the freight depot.'

'He says.'

Chapman shrugged. 'You won't find

many folk in this town want to argue with Brock Powers, even if they don't b'lieve him.'

Rand left his saddle and rifle in the stall, glancing at Chapman, who nodded. 'I'll keep an eye on 'em.'

Grim-faced, the bounty hunter moved away down the aisle, settling the holstered six-gun he had taken from Todd Reason to a more comfortable — and accessible — position.

* * *

Doc Swanson himself answered the door, a napkin tucked into his shirt front, obviously disturbed at supper, or about to begin. He seemed mildly surprised to see Rand.

'Hear The Duke's been beat-up again.'

'We-ell. His injuries could be consistent with a rather brutal beating. In fact, I'm leaning towards that explanation. He doesn't seem to — or want to — remember very clearly.'

'Can I see him, Doc?'

The medic stepped aside and Rand entered. 'Try not to get him too excited. He's recovering, but he is getting on in years now and it takes longer. I believe he said his sixty-third birthday is coming up in a day or two.'

The Duke was the only patient in the small infirmary. There was a bandage around his head, some sutures above a blackened and swollen right eye, a small plaster on his cheek. His left arm was in a sling and when he grinned at his visitor, Rand thought there might be a couple of extra gaps between the old, yellowed teeth, too.

'Who did it, Duke?' asked Rand without preamble, hitching one hip on to the edge of the bed.

'Must've tripped — had a few too many drinks.'

'Where'd you get the money?'

'Aw, here and there. I'm a pretty good panhandler.' He seemed more subdued than usual, his speech thick, likely because of a busted mouth. He

197

grimaced as he tried to get his body into a more comfortable position.

'You got busted ribs, too?'

'Musta landed on a rock when I fell.'

Rand rose and arranged the pillows behind the oldster. Close up he saw how grey the leathery old skin was. 'This looks like a bad one, Duke. Don't gimme eyewash.'

The old, pain-filled eyes lifted to Rand's face. After a moment studying his visitor, Duke said, haltingly, 'My own fault. Had a little trouble in the saloon with a couple hard fellers and like a fool ran to Powers for help. You know, 'Put me in a cell where they can't get at me'. He did, but he kept lookin' at me kind of — queer, like he was sizing me up. Suddenly, he says, he'd been thinking hard about certain things — and figured that maybe you was right: that Feeney did have a pard after all.'

'What made him come around to that?'

Duke was looking at Rand intently

now, his old chest heaving as he breathed. 'Think . . . I did.'

'You convinced him?'

The Duke scratched at a little dried blood on one ear lobe with a broken fingernail. 'Powers is a feller that, once he gets a notion into his head, he convinces himself it's gotta be the right one.'

'I'll go along with that. You said you were drunk — did you let slip something you shouldn't've?'

The Duke frowned, wouldn't hold Rand's gaze. 'Hey! You make it sound like *I* was Feeney's pard!'

'Weren't you, Duke? I hear you did a lot of drinking together — two-three-day benders at a time. Raised a little hell, staying out of town and Powers' reach.'

'Who told you that?' Duke managed to sound indignant.

'Someone who used to see you had decent grub and somewhere warm and dry to sleep it off — the times you weren't already in jail, that is.'

The Duke frowned, started to straighten, then sagged back against the pillow pile. 'You been talking to Georgia Horan.'

Rand nodded. The old man shrugged, quickly grabbing at one shoulder with his good hand. Rand's eyes narrowed. 'Duke, I think you're mighty lucky.'

Duke's one good eye opened as wide as it would go. 'Me? Lucky? You glare-blind or somethin'?'

'Lucky to be still alive, I mean. Someone gave you a mighty bad going-over.'

The oldster didn't speak again for a few minutes and Rand heard his breath wheezing in the heaving chest.

'Georgia — fine woman,' he gasped at last. 'Works the various stage depots all round the Territory — you know? Me and Feen'd hang around the depots she was at — hopin' for a hand-out. We could always get a feed and a drink, even, mebbe a couple of dollars, when she was there. She'd make us set down to a decent meal before she'd let us have a slug of something to keep us

200

going. She savvied neither of us could get through a day without some likker.'

'A good-hearted woman,' Rand agreed, putting his steady gaze on Duke, and seeing how it unsettled him. Just as if he knew what was coming. 'She thinks you and Feeney may've seen that strongbox with the construction company's payroll being loaded on to the stage — she's sure you were at that particular depot at the time.'

Duke smiled crookedly, as much as his battered lips would allow. 'Smart lady, that Georgia. Yeah, we both seen it from where we was sleeping in a hay loft right over the loading dock. The armed guards being there told us that it had to be something big.'

'And you two were still drunk and got the notion that you could make yourselves rich — right?'

'You're pretty damn smart, too.' Duke nodded slowly. 'Yeah. We actually done it! Surprised the hell outta ourselves. Feen held up the stage while I . . . borrowed a couple horses for getaway mounts and held 'em ready in the brush. The booze was wearing off by that time and we were both a bundle of nerves, specially Feen. Was the biggest job he'd ever pulled. After we left the stage stranded by running off the team, we separated, Feen going to some hideout he'd been using, me heading back here.'

'But you arranged to meet later in that dead-end canyon?'

'Yeah, but not for a couple of weeks; we wanted things to die down a little — we were both pretty scared by the time we sobered up an' realized what we'd done.' The Duke watched Rand's face which gave nothing away about his thoughts as he waited patiently for the oldster to continue.

'Ginger had spotted me with the mounts. I seen her in the brush and while I had a bandanna covering my face this old bush of hair kind of gives me away, all that silver and real long, like. But I knew she wouldn't tell anyone.'

'Pushing your luck, weren't you?'

Duke shook his head. 'Not really — she took a shine to me long ago. Reminded her of some uncle who treated her good when she was a kid. That's what she said, anyway. But Riley Duggan used to slip in to see her now and again and I think she took a real shine to him. But they had a fallin'-out, over him going off with one of the other whores in the Shotglass and he belted her. She saw a chance to get back at Riley, told you she heard Feen call his pard by that name — which never happened, of course.'

'Woman scorned, eh?'

'I guess. She never really expected you to track down Riley, but I hear you caught up with him.'

'A near-death experience, Duke, but never mind that part. He's dead now. Tell me about the canyon, when you rendezvoused with Feeney.'

The Duke closed his eyes and swayed a little from the waist up, side to side. Then abruptly he grabbed at his ribs, baring his teeth as the pain knifed through his battered body.

'Take it easy, old-timer. I'm getting you all worked-up. Sorry. Maybe I better come back later.'

The rheumy eyes opened slowly and the shaggy head moved slowly, side to side. 'Time to . . . get it into the open, Chet. Been bothering me plenty.' He swallowed, seemed to be collecting his thoughts.

'We had a place we used to meet, time to time, share a few drinks, give our little benders a decent kick-off, I guess. Well, Feen was drunk when I met him in the canyon — but he was different, somehow. Was only later I figured he wasn't drunk on likker. He'd done something that made him so damned pleased with himself that he was walking on air, just as if he'd put away a bottle of bourbon. Knowing Feen, he could've put away two bottles. But I'm not sure he would've been floating the way he was that day even if he had.'

'Maybe it was just sinking in that he'd pulled off the biggest job of his life,' suggested Rand.

'Yeah!' Duke emphasized the word with a jerk of his head and by slapping his good hand on the bed. 'That's it! I mean, his stint as a robber hadn't got him any more than drinking money, over the years. Now, we'd — *he*'d grabbed enough to buy a whole blamed saloon! But what really gave him his lift was — he was sure he'd been really smart, hid that loot so damn good he reckoned no one would ever find it without help from him. And that included me.'

Rand smiled thinly; it sounded to him like Feeney's brain had been pickled by all the booze he'd put away. But he didn't interrupt The Duke.

'He kept telling me how well he'd hid the money. He wanted me to keep askin' '*Where?*' He was so keyed up about how clever he'd been, he just couldn't pass up the chance to surprise me when the time was right.'

Rand had rolled two cigarettes, gave one to Duke and lit both. Blowing smoke, he watched the oldster through the haze as Duke coughed but dragged as deep as he could without hurting his ribs.

'And the right time was when you met in the canyon?'

Duke nodded, a half-dreamy look on his battered face now. His prune lips compressed so that the blood faded from them momentarily and it was as if he had a white mouth. He blurted out, 'I never murdered Feeney, Chet. I never!'

Rand held the rheumy stare and nodded slightly.

'Feen was damn excited, took real pleasure in keeping me dangling that way. It started to rile me a little. Likely it was the first time he'd ever felt as if he was kingpin. He even said that, finally, he was a real outlaw . . . ' He shook his head slowly. 'Poor old Feen. I never knew that was important to him — after all those years of petty crime I s'pose and now he'd hit the big time.'

'Did he ever tell you or show you where he hid it?'

Rand wanted to keep the old man on the main subject.

'Eh? Think I'd still be here if he had? No. He was really enjoying himself, keeping me on edge and in suspense, but I was getting impatient and I told him to damn well get on with it or I was going. So he said for me to go up on the rim first and make sure no one had followed me to the canyon. He'd have a cup of coffee and if it was all clear, he'd show me where the loot was when I came back down.'

'Teasing you.'

'Yes. He was having himself a good time, making me wait, but it had gone on a bit too long and I cussed him out. *That* even amused him! I grabbed my old Spencer carbine: brought it back from the War. We used it as a prop in some of the short plays we staged when I was touring the theatres. It was still in working order, but pretty well worn, not really safe with that big mule-ear side-hammer but it was the only gun I had.

'Anyway, I went up by a kind of goat track — and I can see you're ahead of me, Chet!' He paused, shaking his head in wonderment at the memory. His voice became raspy, broke on a few words as he spoke. 'I heard Feen's horse whinnying something awful, crawled right out to the edge and seen it swinging its head up and down. There was a snake hanging from its neck. Feen went after it with his knife, slashing like crazy. The snake fell off but the blade hacked into the horse's jugular. Feen loved that old jughead and he dropped to his knees as it fell, hosing blood everywhere. I could hear him crying and like a fool I tried to climb down from the ridge instead of going all the way round to the easy way I'd used comin' up. I fell and the damn rifle went off; that big mule-ear lug on the side hammer must've hit a rock . . . ' The Duke stopped, unable to go on. He cleared his throat, gave Rand a haunted look, eyes glinting. 'He was bendin' over the horse, his back all exposed. I — killed poor old Feeney! The bullet, a big .56 slug, hit him square between the shoulders. I swear, Chet, I just hung there, staring down, couldn't move. Then I seen dust, way out but heading in towards the canyon. It was you, of course. There was nothing I could do for Feeney. I went through his gear fast as I could, hoping to find the loot or some clue about where he'd hid it — it must've taken longer than I thought, 'cause next thing you rode in. I don't really know what I had in mind, then, but I set Feen up between a couple of rocks, stuck his Winchester under his arm and started shooting wild. It scared the hell outta me when you shot him twice in the chest. But it gave me time to get away while you were checking him over . . . '

His voice trailed off and Rand waited but there was no more: the Duke had squeezed himself dry, lightened his conscience, and was now in a mental limbo.

'So you hightailed it back to town, got drunk again, and Powers threw you in the cells.' Rand spoke clearly and matter-of-factly. 'Where he took to you in his usual way.'

Duke nodded dully. 'I was mighty upset, raving on. I must've said something that gave him enough to figure how things'd happened. I guess he's been out there, tearing up that canyon, whenever he can find the time.'

'And in between, keeping you in jail and beating you up, hoping you'd spill something that would put him on to the twelve grand.'

'Yeah. But I've no idea where Feen hid it. No — damn — idea at all, Chet!' He sighed. 'Silly old fool! I know he wasn't trying to do me out of my share, mind, just toying with me, figuring we were safe and he'd have a little fun at my expense that wouldn't hurt, that's all.'

Rand drew on his cigarette, looking levelly at the Duke.' Powers is growing impatient by now, I reckon.'

Duke snorted quietly. 'You could say that — won't believe I dunno where it is. He gimme one helluva working-over this time. Scared himself, I think, thought he'd gone too far ... ' His swollen lips twitched a little. 'I thought so, too, for a spell.'

Rand stood abruptly. 'You better take it easy, Duke. I'll see you later. A few things I need to do.'

He was going out through the door when the oldster called after him, 'Don't you get in no trouble on my account, Chet.'

'No trouble at all, Duke. No trouble at all.'

12

Dead End

Jackie 'Ginger' Holt was in her upstairs room, carefully painting on lip rouge, in preparation for the usual business of the night, when one of the other bar girls, a bleach-haired, overweight veteran called 'Baggie Aggie' opened the door.

Ginger swung away from the mirror when she heard the woman's stertorous breathing, knew Aggie must have run up the stairs — and that meant she had something important to tell.

'Where's the fire?'

Aggie held up a soft, pudgy hand, gulping in her effort to catch enough breath so she could speak.

'It's — R-Riley . . . '

Ginger stiffened, face straightening now. 'What — about him?'

'They got him down to the — under-taker's.'

Ginger's stool clattered as it fell over when she leapt up. '*What!*'

Aggie nodded vigorously. 'That bounty hunter — Rand — brung him in. But Powers won't admit it could be Riley.'

Ginger's hands tightened into fists and she grabbed at herself under her left breast, blood draining from her face. 'Wh-what does that mean? 'Could be' . . . '

Aggie had the grace to blush. 'Well — seems a bullet ricocheted and — hit Riley in the face.'

'Oh, my God!'

Aggie ran forward as Ginger grabbed at the edge of her dressing-table. The older woman righted the stool and eased Ginger down on to it.

'I-I'm sorry, Ginger. Didn't mean to break it to you — this way. Can't really blame the sheriff, though.'

Whitefaced, Ginger looked up, freshly rouged lips a-tremble. 'You've — seen Riley?'

Baggie Aggie hesitated briefly, then nodded. 'I-I went an' looked. Aw, Ginger, I dunno. Think it's Riley. Same sorta hair, though it's stiff with blood. Oh, sorry! He's wearin' that red shirt you bought him — least, I think it's the one . . . '

Ginger stood slowly, trembling visibly. 'Damn, I-I'll have to go see him.'

'Aw, now, wait. I mean . . . hell, Ginger, he ain't pretty — and it might not be him, of course . . . '

But Ginger was already on her way out of the room. Aggie swore under her breath and hurried after her, taking her by the arm.

'I'll come with you.'

Ginger felt sick. Several of the other whores were gathered near the foot of the stairs and she saw the way they were looking at her. They knew it was Riley Duggan in the undertaker's back room!

But she had to see for herself — confirm what she had *done* by telling Rand she had heard Feeney refer to the man holding the getaway mounts as 'Riley'.

Oh, Rile! I-I was mad at you! I never meant . . .

The words crashed around inside her head as Aggie helped her along the boardwalk. The undertaker's building front was the brightest on the street, painted with reds and yellows, a splash of white, and some streaks of green for the sign that read: LOVETT'S UNDERTAKING PARLOUR. WE LOVE OUR WORK.

Ginger pushed right past the unctious Mr Lovett, who was dressed immaculately in frock-coat and dark trousers, with appropriate grey shirt and black tie. But despite the formal attire he looked rather comical, mainly because he was a short, fat, jolly-looking man in his middle years. He spent time each day in front of a mirror trying to perfect a look of genuine sympathy for the bereaved, but so far he had been unsuccessful and it truly bothered him.

'Where is he?' Ginger demanded, her voice tremulous and as Lovett began some stock greeting about grief and the Better World hereafter, Aggie took Ginger's arm and led her through to the back, pushing aside a heavy dark-green curtain. Lovett had already laid out Riley Duggan in a cheap pine box but when he made to come in, Aggie glared and pushed him out through the curtain.

'I understand,' he said in his carefully practised mournful voice. 'The bereaved always need some time alone with their dear, departed loved ones.'

'Just wait out there!' Aggie snapped and turned to see Ginger leaning into the coffin.

Riley had had a lot of the blood washed away but the bullet damage still made it difficult to determine the original features. Aggie caught Ginger as her legs gave way, helped her to a chair. The younger woman was breathing heavily and fast, her face whiter than Aggie had ever seen it.

Her lips moved and the older whore leaned down. quickly. 'Sorry, dear. Didn't hear . . . '

'It — it's him!' Ginger croaked. 'Oh, Lord, I got him murdered by that damn bounty hunter!'

Aggie heard the rising anger and wondered if she should feed it; maybe it would be better than the overwhelming grief. At the same time, maybe there was a better way to ease Ginger's shock.

'It — it's hard to be sure, love. I mean . . . '

Ginger lifted her tear-stained face. 'You were sure when you came to get me!'

Aggie backed away from that approach. 'Well, I did think I recognized him, but we could be wrong.'

Ginger shook her head, starting to regain control. 'No. I know Riley, all of him, and if I have to look at other . . . parts of him, I-I'll know for sure. But, dammit, Aggie, I'm already sure! That hard bastard killed him!'

'Yeah. Rand! Says he ain't really a

bounty hunter. But a man's *gotta* be a killer if he goes after another man just for the price on his head! A cold-blooded killer! Son of a *bitch*!'

Ginger had her cry, sobbing, shoulders shaking, Aggie awkwardly slipping one of her flabby arms about her, making soothing sounds.

'He'll get his one day, Ginger. You-you could even tell Brock Powers it ain't Riley. Spoil things for Rand.'

Ginger lifted her puffy, wet face and stared at her friend. Slowly, it sank in.

'Yes! By God, Ag, that's what I'll do! I'll make sure Rand don't get a red cent from Riley!' Then her face took on a sly look that made it truly ugly for a few moments, causing Aggie to step back. 'But maybe *I*'ll have something else for him, a kind of bonus he won't be expectin'!'

Aggie's jaw dropped. 'Aw, now wait up, love! Don't you go an' do anythin' foolish . . . '

The green curtain rustled. 'I trust I'm not intruding, ladies, but I heard

218

your grief and if I can be of assistance . . . ?'

Ginger stood abruptly, her jaw hardening as she mopped at her face with her sodden handkerchief.

'Get out of the way, you hypocritical son of a bitch!' She thrust the startled undertaker aside, wrenched the heavy green curtain back and paused before stepping out of the viewing room. 'And put him in a decent coffin! The best you've got — and — and send me the bill!'

She stormed out, and Aggie hurried after her, wondering if she should point out that demanding a better coffin and offering to pay for it might make folk wonder — specially if she denied the body was not that of Riley Duggan.

Then she stopped in her tracks.

Chet Rand was coming out of the street where Doc Swanson had his infirmary.

* * *

Doc Swanson was enjoying his dessert of prunes and custard, his wife taking the used dishes out to the kitchen, when all at once, he felt a strange sensation — nothing he could actually put a finger on, but he suddenly sensed another presence in the room. It had never happened to him before and his heart gave a lurch as he spun swiftly in his chair, spilling the last spoonful of dessert on the clean tablecloth his wife had laid earlier for the evening meal. But he didn't even notice.

The Duke was clinging to the door frame, clothes and one bandage hanging loosely on his emaciated frame. The doctor whipped off his napkin and hurried to him, helping the oldster to an overstuffed chair. His wife came hurrying in and asked,

'Will I bring some coffee, Lucas?'

'He needs something stronger than coffee, woman. Pour him half a glass of whiskey from the decanter.' As she started to question the wisdom of this, he snapped: 'Just get it, will you!' Then, immediately contrite, he said in a gentler voice, 'I'm sorry, dear — didn't mean to snap. But our friend here is in urgent need of a stimulant. I don't know how he's managed to get this far without help.'

She hurried to a sideboy and splashed amber liquid into a glass with a diamond pattern etched into it.

The Duke came alive when he saw the whiskey. He lifted a shaky hand to guide it unerringly to his mouth, gulping greedily. He would have swallowed it all in one long draught if the doctor hadn't pulled the glass away.

'Now, just take it easy, Duke! What on earth are you doing out of bed, anyway?'

The reply was a series of raspy gasps but they were intelligible to the doctor whose ear had long been attuned to the mutterings of the sick and semiconscious.

'Rand's gonna need help. Or he'll get himself killed — all on account of me.'

'What're you talking about, man?' He

felt Duke's forehead, looked into his eyes.

'Ah, quit that! it ain't fever, Doc! Chet's gone after Jerry Halstead and Lew. They're layin' for him.'

'How does this affect you?'

Duke stared back, mouth tight, then gestured to the glass. Doc hesitated, then let him have the remains of the whiskey. Duke smacked his old, blood-less lips appreciatively.

'I reckon he's getting 'em out of the way first. Then he'll go after Powers.'

'What? He can't go gunning for the sheriff! No matter how much of an arrogant bully he may be, Brock Powers is the duly elected law and — '

'He's a loco mongrel! *That*'s why Rand's going after him. Chet's a decent man, Doc. He won't stand by and see someone who can't fight back get beating after beating from the likes of Powers.'

'I know he's — protective of you, Duke, But — '

'Doc! Main thing is Lew and Jerry

are laying for Rand! Most of the town knows — even Powers. And he won't lift a finger to stop 'em.'

'Brock wouldn't allow that sort of thing!'

'He hates Rand's guts, Doc. He don't need a reason — he's just that measly kind of cheapjack.'

'Well, what d'you expect me to do?'

'Get me some crutches and help me get to that saloon. Oh, and I want to borrow that fancy pearl-handled lady's gun Flora Kelso gave you in payment for fixing her husband up that time after the buckboard crash.'

'You're crazy, you old fool!'

'I'm goin' anyway, Doc. Might need a couple more belts from your decanter, but you ain't gonna stop me. C'mon, Doc! It's me birthday! Be generous.'

* * *

'Ginger!' Aggie called urgently. As the younger girl slowed, looked over her shoulder, Aggie pointed towards Rand.

'Hurry up and go inside!'

'No! He's just the man I want to see!'

There was a sob in her voice, but it was steadier and had a harder sound than Aggie had expected. She hurried up to stand beside Ginger as Rand came on to the boardwalk and touched a hand to his hat brim.

'Howdy, ladies,' he said, nodding to Aggie, but giving most of his attention to Ginger. 'I — er — want to tell you I'm sorry about the way things worked out with Riley. But he near-killed me and then he and Blake came after me to finish the job. It was a square shoot-out in the end.'

'Oh, and that'll bring him back, will it?' demanded Aggie angrily, but Ginger put out a hand and touched her on the arm.

She put her gaze on Rand. 'Why're you sorry?'

'I've only found out since that you and Riley — were good friends. If you hadn't told me — '

'Shut up, damn you!' snapped Aggie

protectively. 'Don't you think she's upset enough!'

She broke off as Ginger suddenly snapped and lunged at the startled Rand, slapping wildly at his face and head and body, screaming invective, trying to claw his eyes out.

He ducked and weaved and fought to get away. Aggie couldn't hold her, although she might not have been really trying; then Rand poked a stiffened finger into Ginger's midriff and she gagged, stopped dead, fighting for breath.

Rand, panting, straightened his hat, and bent down to rub briskly at his shins where she had kicked him.

Folk on the boardwalks, on their way to supper or taking a stroll in the balmy evening, grinned: it wasn't often an angry whore put on a public show.

Aggie held Ginger and helped her slowly straighten up, glaring at Rand. 'You better get out of here! You've done enough. *More* than enough.'

'Ginger, I am truly sorry,' he said. He

nodded briefly and stepped around the whores, making for the saloon.

'Oh, sure!' Ginger said bitterly. 'You're sorry — but you still want the bounty! Well, you won't get it! Hear?'

Rand slowed, then continued on his way.

Ginger had her breath back now and took a shaky step after him but Aggie steadied her.

'Let him go, love; someone'll fix him sooner or later. Jerry and Lew've been waiting for him to come back to town, you know, so maybe it'll be sooner. They're all ready — '

'Where's he going?'

Aggie looked up and saw that Rand hadn't made for the batwings as she had thought. He walked past the front of the saloon and turned down the alley running beside it on the north side. Ginger's grip tightened on Aggie's arm.

'He's going in the side door!'

'Won't help him. Jerry's waiting, and Lew's been polishing his sawed-off for days.'

Ginger suddenly started forward, running towards the batwings. 'But Jerry's waiting at the *other* door!'

Aggie frowned, hearing but not immediately understanding Ginger's words. Then she did: Jerry Halstead was sitting at his corner table, as he had been day after day since recovering from his gunshot wounds, waiting for Rand. If Rand entered by the *north* side door, opposite where Jerry waited, he would have the advantage: Jerry's attention would be on the side door nearest his table. It was the door used most often by saloon patrons who didn't enter by the batwings.

Panting, Ginger staggered into the smoke and noise of the bar room and headed towards the foggy corner where Jerry was pouring himself whiskey from the half-empty bottle, his six-gun resting on the table near at hand.

'Jerry! Jerry!' she called, pointing to the side door across the room. 'Rand's coming in that way! Quick!'

Halstead snapped his head up, leapt

to his feet so suddenly that his thighs caught the edge of the table and sent the bottle and glasses flying. Others who had heard the girl crowded away from the side door she had indicated.

Lew at the bar, no bandage on his hand now, stared at Ginger, then reached beneath the counter, groping for the sawn-off shotgun he had hidden there.

Jerry glanced towards him and Lew made an impatient gesture at the north side door, just as it opened — fast.

Rand came in, crouching, took in the hasty retreat of drinkers and Jerry standing there at his table, still stunned by the girl's shouting at him. His cool gaze flitted across Ginger as Aggie hurried up to the girl and pulled her back.

As Jerry snatched up his Colt, the twin hammers of Lew's shotgun made a loud noise cocking. Rand dived for the floor as it thundered and a spray of buckshot tore into the door. Slivers raked his arm, piercing his shirt as he rolled over and his Colt blasted. From low down, Jerry's falling table intercepted Rand's bullet, sending splinters flying, some stinging Jerry's neck and jaw. Startled — *frightened* now, Halstead turned, loosing off one wild shot, then ran for the door nearest his table.

Rand rolled to his knees as Lew lifted the reloaded shotgun. He triggered, threw himself sideways as his lead smashed the mirror and sent bottles crashing to the floor. Lew fired one barrel and leapt over the counter, shouting after Jerry as the man crashed out into the night. Lew, mouth twisting, ran at Rand, throwing down confidently this time.

Rand hit the floor, rolling, hearing the shotgun roar behind him as he flopped on to his back, wrenched around on his belly and put two fast shots into Lew's chest.

The man was still falling as Chet jumped up and raced out into the night past the swinging south-side door.

Lead seared past his ear, slammed

into the saloon wall. He flattened, dropped to one knee, fumbling fresh cartridges from his belt. He heard running feet as, hand shaking, he took time to reload the pistol.

Jerry was going down the alley, it sounded like. Rand crouched as he made his way along the wall, feeling ahead with his left hand. A crate clattered and he ducked, figuring it might be a decoy, deliberately kicked over so as to get his attention. He held his fire but Jerry was impatient and triggered two more shots in Rand's general direction.

Then he ran, dodging out of the alley through a large hole in the saloon fence and across the yard, weaving between the dark shapes of empty beer kegs and rotting crates. And empty bottles.

Jerry didn't see them ahead and blundered into a small stack. They fell with a shattering clatter and he picked himself up, in a panicky sweat now. He let out a wild curse as he made for the front of the big building.

Rand homed in on the breaking glass, glimpsed Jerry as he lunged past a side window, the shaft of dull orange light just catching him. Rand held his fire, picked his way past the broken glass, then sprinted down the way Jerry had gone.

It opened out on to Springer Street and he slowed as he approached, but had been running so hard that he skidded a couple of feet beyond the saloon wall before he could stop.

Jerry Halstead stepped out of the deep shadow, shooting. The bullet was so close that it plucked at the loose cloth of the right sleeve on Rand's shirt, twisting him a little so that Jerry's second slug burned past his cheek.

His shot came so close to Jerry's last one that it covered the sound of his own. Halstead stiffened, lifting to his toes, tried to bring up his gun. Rand fired one more time and Jerry went spinning down to the dust, thrashing briefly, before going still for ever.

Nothing seemed to move on the

street, except the drifting gunsmoke.

Then folk began appearing out of doorways, from where they had hurriedly crouched behind rainwater butts when the gunfight had spilled on to the street; some leaned out of windows, craning to see who was lying in the dust, and who was hunched over, reloading a hot pistol in the alley mouth next to the saloon.

Men came thrusting through the batwings, eager, yet wary, and Ginger pushed through hurriedly, followed by a panting Aggie. The men gave way reluctantly as the whores ran to the edge of the veranda.

Ginger was white-faced as she saw that Rand was the only one standing. With a cry way back in her throat, she whirled towards the nearest gawking drinker and snatched his Colt from his holster.

'Hey! What the . . . ?'

Whining, she lifted it in both hands, awkwardly trying to cock the hammer, then the owner of the gun, grabbed her wrist and twisted the weapon free.

'The hell you think you're doin'?'

Ginger was sobbing now and leaned on the rail, Aggie trying to comfort her.

Then Sheriff Brock Powers came running up, six-gun in hand, taking in Jerry's body. Rand had just finished reloading.

'Kinda got you red-handed, eh, *bounty hunter!*' Powers said with satisfaction, lifting his Colt. 'Drop that gun!'

Ginger suddenly came to life, leaned far over the rails. 'Brock! Brock! It's not Riley! That man this — this murderous bastard brought in isn't Riley Duggan!' She actually smiled at Rand. 'Don't pay him no bounty!'

Powers laughed, nodded, telling her he savvied what she was about. 'You hear that, Rand? You're in a lot of trouble, mister . . . '

'Not as much as you,' Rand said, cocking his Colt.

The sheriff, in turning to look at Ginger had unwittingly lowered his gun, let it wander: it was pointing nowhere in particular.

But Rand's gun was covering him. 'Drop it, Powers,' Rand advised quietly. The sheriff hesitated, but decided not to be foolish. He let his Colt fall to the ground, then reared back as Rand stepped towards him in two long strides.

Rand's left hand stabbed out. Powers jerked as his badge was torn from his shirt and flung away into the street. The sheriff frowned. 'The hell're you doing?'

'Without the badge you're just another ranny, Powers. No authority, nothing more than an ordinary man.'

'You think I need a badge to run this town?'

'I wouldn't know — nor care.' Rand holstered his Colt. 'When you were beating up The Duke in his cell and I told you to try it on me you said you'd get around to it. Well, the time's here. Right now! What d'you say, Powers? Want to try your luck?'

The crowd murmured and some men

immediately started laying bets as to who would be the winner.

The sheriff, dead sober, studied Rand's face, knew he could not dodge this challenge — nor did he want to. With the speed of a striking snake, and without signalling his intentions in any way, he threw himself at Rand bodily, taking the bounty hunter by surprise.

They went down thrashing, Rand underneath. Hard, experienced fists hammered at his face and upper chest. A knee drove into his belly; Powers half-raised himself then slammed down again, smashing the breath from Rand.

The shouts of the crowd faded and the night seemed to close down like a sack pulled over Rand's head. He jarred with the impact of a barrage of blows, felt himself going away.

'Who — you say — was in trouble?' gasped Powers, raising a fist preparatory to smashing it into the middle of Rand's face.

But the taunting words broke through Rand's fading consciousness and his strong survival instinct cut in. He wrenched his head aside as the big fist whistled down. If it had landed it would have squashed his nose, smashed his cheekbone, loosened almost every tooth in his head.

But it skimmed past, setting one ear burning and ringing, then drove into the gravel of the street.

Brock Powers howled with the pain in his knuckles and automatically reared upright, snatching the injured hand to his chest. Rand swept his legs around and kicked the sheriff's legs from under him. Powers thudded to the dust and Rand threw himself atop him. But the sheriff was experienced in rough and tumble and his own instincts set him writhing out from under before Rand could pin him.

Lying on his back, he brought up his boots as Rand came at him again. They caught Rand in the chest and heaved him back almost two yards. Both men staggered up at about the same time, circled each other warily, crouched, fists up, ready for attack or protection.

Powers kicked up some gravel and dust and Rand jumped to one side, leapt in and slammed a savage blow against the sheriff's kidneys. The lawman's legs buckled and he staggered but he didn't go down. He turned sharply, swinging a backhanded blow that took Rand by surprise, and smashed him on the side of the jaw.

He stumbled and went down to one knee before he could get his balance. Powers surged in, fists swinging from hip level as he pummelled Rand's head and shoulders. Chet dropped suddenly and Powers staggered as he swung a blow that didn't find a target. He almost fell as Rand rammed upwards, the top of his head catching the sheriff under the jaw. The teeth clacked together and Powers fell sideways, putting out a hand to keep from going down all the way.

Rand kicked the supporting arm away and the sheriff sprawled. But he was tough and, dazed and hurt though he was, he rolled away and Rand's swinging boot whistled past his head. He jumped to all fours and bulled back like a charging buffalo.

His flailing arms encircled Rand's hips and the sheriff roared with effort as he lifted the man and, with a massive grunt, threw him at the wooden steps of the saloon.

Spectators hurriedly thrust and jostled each other in an effort to get out of the way.

It might have broken Rand's back had he landed across those steps, but Powers wasn't quite as strong as he had hoped and the bounty hunter fell short by a couple of feet. He still skidded hard into the bottom step and one shoulder jarred and went numb. But he kept his head out of the way and, dazed, lights whirling behind his eyes, he rolled.

Powers lumbered in, boot swinging at his head. He missed and fought for balance as Rand pulled himself up by the edge of the steps, moved on to the bottom tread and, with the advantage of these eight inches or so of extra height he drove a straight left into the lawman's face.

Powers wasn't ready for that, and Rand's knuckles cracked against his temple so hard the man did half a cartwheel before he crashed to hands and knees. Rand ran at him, got a kick into the man's side and moved the big body a couple of feet. Powers grunted but he was moving a lot slower now with the breath hammered out of him, and he caught a second kick that felt like a Missouri mule had let him have both rear feet.

He folded and crawled away, gagging, a sick man.

Rand paused to get his breath, feeling all the hurt from the numerous blows he had taken. Irritably, he wiped blood out of his right eye where it trickled down from a gash above the brow. This was no time to rest: he had to follow his advantage, and fast.

Powers was stumbling away from him but Rand stalked him and the man ran into the edge of the yelling crowd. The men there jostled him and thrust him back, a few giving way, but most taking the chance to get a little of their own back on this arrogant bully who had ruled this town for far too long.

They thrust the sheriff back into Rand's path and the men collided, floundered apart, then, both wanting to finish the other, drew together again.

Powers' fists came up smartly as he crouched, hurting and ready for revenge. His face was dripping blood and Rand looked little better as he circled warily, searching for an opening that Powers had no intention of giving him: the sheriff tracked his every move, set for defence or attack.

'Get on with it!' someone yelled, impatient to see yet more blood and bruised or torn flesh.

'Yeah — quit waltzin' around!'

'Don't stop now. It's just gettin' interestin'.'

'Throw a bucket of water on 'em!' someone suggested. 'They're in shock.'

It was doubtful that either man heard the taunts, but, suddenly, as if with one mind, they closed in a flurry of fists and grunts, jarring bodies, dodging, crouching to get under the other's guard, long-stepping to dart several lightning fast blows before retreating out of range.

Powers' boot slipped and he fought to keep from going down to one knee. Rand took instant advantage, rammed in and hooked the man savagely in the ribs on the side he knew he had hurt earlier. The sheriff folded, gagging, clawing at Rand for support.

The bounty hunter lifted a knee into the man's chest and, as Powers straightened, measured him with three rapid, mauling straight lefts that had the sheriff back-peddling quickly.

While he was off-balance, Rand closed and hooked a right into his midriff, followed by a whistling left upper-cut into the descending face, followed by another right that cracked against Powers' jaw like a cleaver hacking into a side of beef.

The lawman's feet left the ground and he crumpled like a rag doll with the stuffing pulled out. His face bounced off gravel and he moaned once, half-rolling on to his back, then flopping again, face down, spinning into oblivion.

Rand fought to keep his balance, breathing hard, wiping his battered face on his sweat-soaked, ragged sleeve.

The crowd was silent, awed: no one had seen Big Brock Powers stretched out unconscious in the middle of the main street, or anywhere else for that matter. They stared at the sight, flicking gazes at the slowly recovering Rand every so often.

Then Ginger, pale and shaking, pushed through and stood in front of him, leaning forward, her face ugly with bitter rage.

'You *still* won't get the bounty!' she choked.

Rand stared back, then nodded slightly and shrugged; let her have the last word if it made her feel better. But he knew that what she had to live with would keep her awake for many nights to come.

The crowd watched her walk away, shakily and sobbing, Aggie steadying her as well as she could.

Bets were paid and men called to one another, milling about. Then suddenly The Duke was standing before Rand, who blinked as he saw the oldster on crutches, holding out a neckerchief towards him.

The old-timer grinned as Rand took the cloth, wiped away some of the blood and grinned back. Duke gripped his crutches carefully, and surprised everyone by prancing in a fair imitation of an Indian powwow victory dance, including wild war cries.

Doc Swanson hurriedly stepped forward and steadied The Duke before he got too carried away. He glanced at the unconscious sheriff, then addressed Rand.

'It may be prudent for you to leave town fairly quickly, I think, Mr Rand.

Our sheriff is a rather unforgiving person.'

Rand nodded, chest still heaving from the exertions of the fight. 'Lasky's waterhole is far from Powers' bailiwick, Doc. I've got a temporary job there. Maybe permanent, ain't sure yet.' He turned to look at Duke who was just now getting his breath back. 'Where'd you learn to dance like that, Duke?'

'You wouldn't b'lieve me if I told you,' Duke cackled and Doc Swanson, still holding the oldster's arm, shook his head slowly.

'Never ceases to surprise me, this man. Sixty-three years old today he tells me, been beaten within an inch of his life, and still can manage to dance like an Indian at a powwow — brief though it was.'

Rand grinned after wiping blood from his mouth. He nodded towards Power's slowly stirring form.

'Happy birthday, Duke.'

Duke grinned with his gapped teeth.

'Thanks, Chet. Best birthday present I've ever had.'

Other titles in the
Linford Western Library:

HOMBRE'S VENGEANCE

Toots J. Johnson

After witnessing his father's murder at the hands of cattle baron Dale Bryant, fifteen-year-old Zachariah Smith grows up fast. Struggling alone to survive fully occupies his mind — until he meets two of Bryant's other victims. He realises that he must join the fight for justice and avenge his father's death, knowing that lead will fly and he will probably die trying to stop Bryant. But now Zac is a man, and it is time for the hombre's vengeance!

IRON EYES IS DEAD

Rory Black

Desert Springs was an oasis that drew the dregs of Texas down into its profitable boundaries. Among the many ruthless characters, there was none so fearsome as the infamous bounty hunter, Iron Eyes. He had trailed a dangerous outlaw right into the remote settlement. But Iron Eyes was wounded: shot up with arrow and bullet after battling with a band of Apaches. As the doctor fought to save him, was the call true that Iron Eyes was dead?

TAKE THE OREGON TRAIL

Eugene Clifton

Thousands of men had taken the trail to the west looking for a new beginning — many didn't make it. Adam Trant had also set out on the Oregon Trail — but he was looking for an old enemy. The hunt took him to a savage wilderness and matched him against deadly marauders. Adam was ready to die, as long as he succeeded in his quest. However, he wasn't ready for the unpredictable force of the love of a woman.

FOOL'S PLAY

Carl Williams

Royce rides into Jawbone looking for a doctor, but finds trouble. Living by the gun can he expect anything else? He signs on with land baron Yale Jamerson, hoping for a job that will leave his conscience clear. However, when Jamerson plans to dam the river and charge road tolls, the townspeople revolt. Forced to choose between his livelihood and his conscience, Royce must decide which path to take. Will it lead to a showdown with his closest friend?

THE VENOM OF VALKO

Michael D. George

The bounty for the capture of the Valko Kid is a fortune, drawing the lowest of the low to try and claim it. On one bright moonlit night, Sheriff Colby Masters leads his posse to a narrow canyon ridge to await Valko, who is heading for the town of War Smoke. Suddenly below them, thundering through the canyon, rides a horseman clad in black and riding a magnificent white stallion . . . Soon they will all taste *The Venom of Valko* . . .